**ABOUT T**

After leaving Sedbergh School and serving an apprenticeship with the Royal Insurance Company in Liverpool, Bill Richardson joined the Foreign Department and was sent to India. He spent some forty years overseas in six different countries, plus a spell in London before settling down in Ross-on-Wye, in Herefordshire.

Along the way, he developed a fondness for writing, confining this to a variety of short stories and articles published at random.

The most vivid memories that came back to him, aided by old diaries and other souvenirs, were of India, and from these he gradually compiled the nostalgic stories presented in **An English Rose** ...

# THE ENGLISH ROSE

### and other
### Stories of British India

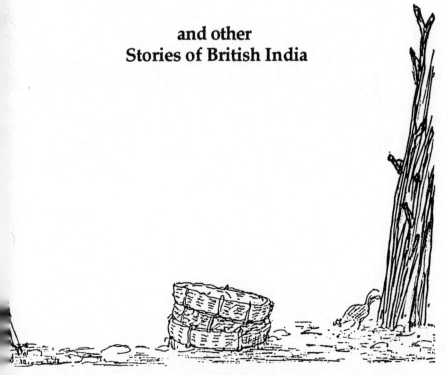

# THE ENGLISH ROSE

**and other
Stories of British India**

William Richardson

A Square One Publication

First published in 1993 by
Square One Publications
Sansome Place, Worcester WR1 1UA


© William Richardson 1993
ISBN: 1 872017 73 8


British Library Cataloguing-In-Publication  Data
A catalogue record for this book
is available from the British Library

Typeset in Palatino 12 point on 13 by Square One Publications
Printed by Antony Rowe, Chippenham, England

To

Angela and Rosemary

my two

"Lights of Asia"

# CONTENTS

# PREFACE

Of all the territories and islands which formed the huge area of the British Colonial Empire in its heyday, not only was India a large and complete unit, vastly populated, but it radiated glamour, bred prestige, and demanded the very best qualities of education and breeding from Britons who found themselves, by accident or design, deputed there as Rulers, keepers of law and order, or honest brokers in Trade and Industry.

Years later it has become fashionable in some quarters to see the lives led by these representatives of the Imperial power as a round of privilege, ease, comfort and opulence in an atmosphere of arrogant pride and snobbery accompanied by an attitude towards the native population of the sub-continent, from the high-born to the lowest caste, ranging from off-handed patronage to harsh contempt and even cruelty. Those who were, despite many disadvantages, lucky enough to be there need make no apology to disgruntled latter-day interpreters of what they call human rights. Much less might they recall, over a period long enough to be credible, any notable occasion of the infringement of such rights except at the hands of some Princes or other despotic Rulers or autocrats of Indian blood.

As in any ordered society the world over, those who found themselves on the wrong side of the Law were there by the nature of their own actions, deliberate or misguided.

Thus my stories are about the times that were. Then, to be in some worthy capacity in India and entitled to wander there without let or hindrance was the most natural thing in the world. Just as natural as for the cook to catch smallpox or typhus, for one's best friend to nearly die of typhoid, for one's favourite newly-weds' first-born to succumb to malaria, for cholera and bubonic plague to thrive on contaminated food and water, and for dysentery, sprue and B-coli to be everyday parlour talk. As for dengue, prickly heat, diarrhoea and anaemia, these were no more than commonplace inconveniences.

Notwithstanding all this, India had its incomparable scenery and abundant wildlife to complement an allure and a magical history of its own which still gripped the hearts and feelings of all but the most insensitive of expatriates right up to the end of the last decade before Independence.

Politics then took over, the armed forces of British India were disbanded, Viceroys and Provincial Governors disappeared and with them the bulk of top Civil servants. Pakistan came into being, followed by Bangladesh, and the map of India was redrawn. A number of Britons, unable to visualise any other kind of life, stayed on.

# THE ENGLISH ROSE

The time when he had first arrived in India to take up a post in the Bombay branch of a prominent Insurance Company made an indelible impression on Harry Walters. Fortunately it had not been the hottest time of the year and there was so much to take in and arrange, from finding somewhere to live, joining Clubs and getting to know other members of the large European community, to learning how the business ran, that the information he had stored up before he went out and the painstaking advice of various well wishers scarcely found a place in his mind.

Connections did though, and instrumental in getting Walters into a "Chummery" was an old friend from home in the cotton business, Paul Wilson, who had found a "Bearer" for him and, in a way, taken him under his wing.

"There are a few dos and don'ts, Harry", said Paul at an early social evening in the chummery as he mechanically undid the bottom button of Walter's waistcoat, but otherwise eyeing him approvingly.

"As I told you, though white dinner jackets are worn in Calcutta, the evening dress here is a black DJ and white cotton trousers, and really I'd get a cummerbund rather than that waistcoat! The "Dharzi" I sent you to seems to have done the trousers all right. How many pairs did you get?"

"Three."

"Calling cards?" asked Paul.

Walters produced one. It had the office address, but no designation of position.

"Good, not only would you never get to Government

House without that, but all burra sahibs, neighbours and so forth look on them as the only proper form of introduction."

"I've stuck a few in boxes already," said Walters looking and feeling quite pleased about it.

"Right, now about the Indians. You don't shake hands with the ordinary ones. Parsee business acquaintances and westernised Hindus and Moslems, yes, but the others you say 'Salaam' to and do a sort of half salute."

"I've noticed that," Walters said.

"Taking girls out or asking them round like the two who are here now is fairly formal," Wilson motioned his hand limply in their direction, "but not too bad. Only thing is that being seen too often with the same girl on one's first contract is a bit risky."

"Why's that?" asked Walters.

"Well, 'Chokras' of our age are actively discouraged from having ideas about a wife before they are ripe for it. Not only are we not supposed to be able to afford it, but the problems of health and children and the "Hot Weather' require care and experience."

"What about chaps who have fiancées or something at home?"

"Well, yes, that's a bit of a shame," Paul admitted. "Not many people get away with less than a four year contract, and when they get home on leave the girl's affections are often elsewhere. The result is that most chaps are about 28 before they take the plunge, and I suppose that's the general idea."

Harry Walters looked at the girls further down the glassed-in upper verandah of the bungalow and thought that he would prefer a wider selection. He hoped they weren't too representative of the renowned "Fishing

Fleet".

"Oh, and of course," Paul had almost forgotten. "You must not, on any account, mix with 'Chi chis'.

So Walters had wanted to know what these were.

"Anglo-Indians or country-born people," explained Paul. "It's their sing-song accent. Mostly they are on the Railways or in the Post Office or something like that. Also in shops where some of the girls in Whiteaway Laidlaws or the Army & Navy Stores are rather attractive; and now some are coming into offices as shorthand-typists."

"Any in yours?" asked Walters.

"We haven't any. Two East Indian Christians take notes. They're good, these chaps."

"Same with us," said Paul. "Well those are the main things. We'd better do some fraternising."

Three Cold Weathers later Walters found himself pretty well established in the community. He had acquired a 1932 'Opel' car for 1200 rupees, a good reputation in all the popular sports, and membership of the Yacht Club. He'd had jaundice and dengue fever, but nothing worse. Sports, and good company in the course of two different chummeries, filled most of his leisure hours.

In fact he found himself managing all right. For instance people who had shacks at Juhu Beach held fairly open house at weekends, and now that he had a car he joined in some good frolics there, nurses and well vetted other local girls included, met at the occasional Hospital dance.

Walters met a few members of the 'fishing fleet' at parties or at Government House, some of whom were quite outstandingly pretty, but they played very hard to get and were expensive to cultivate. When asked to do anything they would whip out a diary and thumb through a fortnight of pages of dates.

One girl who had come out this Cold Weather nonetheless bothered Walters. Her father was a Captain in the Royal Indian Navy on whom at sometime Walters had dropped a card. He got asked to the first party for her, which was followed by an afternoon of tennis. Three of Walters' friends were at both. Paul Wilson wasn't one of them. He remained the doyen of Walters' first chummery on Pali Hill where newly arrived chokras graduated in etiquette.

At the tennis party the girl, whose name was Mary Cameron, out of a long dress and in a short white skirt, revealed her full charms.

Not quite nineteen years old, of medium height, which brought her about up to Walters' chin, she had a figure which was neither voluptuous nor buxom, but something in between and positively mouth watering.

Her features were regular, her face quite full, and above her very blue eyes she had shoulder length almost gossamery natural fair hair. But what almost floored Walters, after three years in India, was her complexion; it was flawless, a satin white skin and rose pink cheeks which didn't colour up more than half a shade as she dashed round the court. Such perfection couldn't in any way be artificial in this light.

Walters breathed to his friends over a mid-set 'nimbu pani': "She's just like an English Rose!" And the name stuck, although the English Rose was undeniably Scots, and had a gentle Banffshire accent.

About 6.30 pm they all left the Queen's Road tennis courts, and Walters and the three other men, Jack

Rawson who worked in an advertising firm, Bill Horley in Grindlays Bank, and 'Lanky' Newton, another Insurance man, went to the Bombay Gymkhana Club to shower, change, and have a drink. Harry Walters and Lanky decided to eat a cheap meal at Cornaglias and then go to the Regal Cinema.

The English Rose and her friend, Margaret, daughter of the Scots manager of the National Bank of India, made off home to prepare for a party somewhere.

Walters hadn't read very much about India before he went out there, but he believed that the age old religions had endowed the Country with spiritual qualities of a unique kind and that strange powers could really be evoked by saddhus and similar holy men. He had determined to find out more about those sort of things, but in the daily business and social round of Bombay it rather surprised him that no-one he met showed much interest, much less were they able to say where reliable information could be obtained; and then there was the language difficulty.

Some business firms offered salary bonuses to employees freshly out from home who would study and gain diplomas in Hindustani or Urdu, but most people contented themselves with a working knowledge of Bombay 'Bhat' to be able to converse with their servants and get around well enough. This was gained at the hands of a 'Munshi' who would come along to the chummery a couple of evenings a week.

Walters joined in this, but, being good at languages, he went a bit further and got the munshi to expand more than usual.

The munshi, Ranjibhai Desai, after overcoming his initial surprise, showed himself ready to answer

Walters' questions about the power of mind over body and the healing accomplished by holy men with their incantations and herbal remedies. In fact many sections of the Indian native population still relied on the efficacity of the latter, not always to their advantage.

Mr Desai said that there was a 'Rishi' living in a cave beyond Thana some miles out of Bombay and that this man would pay attention to people who visited him if their desire was genuine and not from mere curiosity or to scoff.

"What about Europeans?" Walters asked.

"The same, Sahib."

"But wouldn't it be more difficult for me coming from another civilisation? And how does this Rishi distinguish people and their attitudes?"

"Excuse me, but that is foolish question, Sahib. The Rishi will not open his door to an unbeliever."

Walters thought about the cave having a door, but decided to let it go. He asked the munshi for general directions and thanked him.

He told Lanky Newton about his thoughts of finding out a little of what lay behind some aspects of mystical India one evening at the chummery on Cumballa Hill they shared with Bill Horley. Lanky had been out a year longer than Walters and these days could think of little else but his pending home leave. He was tall, with what is known as a good leg for a boot, to match his cavalry moustache, red like his hair, in front of a good-natured rubicund face. Good natured he was, so not the sort to pour cold water on Walters' enthusiasms.

"Of course there is something in it, Harry," Lanky commented. "It doesn't hold much place in towns on the coast like here and Calcutta and Madras, where we are more in touch with Western countries and ideas, for obvious reasons. To all these University students and modernists it is old-fashioned and reactionary, but go nearer the foothills of the Himalayas, or to Benares or something like the Kumbh Mela at Allahabad, or to any of the hundreds of Ashrams up-country, and nothing has changed."

"Naturally I don't want to be a practitioner of Yoga or anything," Walters replied, "even if I had the time, but I'd like to try and find out about the real thing first hand while I'm here in India."

"Then get to know the Rishi and see what happens," said Lanky.

It was quite a good picture at the Regal Cinema which, being new, had a rather hit and miss, but reasonable, air-conditioning plant and no rats running in and out of the stalls on a hunt for popcorn and peanuts. Walters and Lanky made it back home to the chummery in the 'Opel' without incident.

Next day Walters got an invitation at the office from Capt. and Mrs Cameron to a large Birthday party for the English Rose at his shore establishment in Ballard Estate. Lanky and Bill Horley were also invited, as Walters found when he got home in the evening for dinner. But between then and leaving the office he had a tennis four on at the Gymkhana. On one of the other courts he spotted the English Rose, luscious as ever, knocking up with Margaret James, and straightaway he began to lose concentration and let down his partner, a rather elderly but competitive director of the Port Trust, by unnecessary double faults.

Walters was annoyed with himself. Hadn't he vowed, after the sage advice given to him by Paul Wilson, to sublimate his feelings for the opposite sex by actively pursuing the many opportunities for sport, and do his chasing of birds in a literal way with a twelve bore round a jheel in the cooling light of dawn? Once you start this game, he reflected, you are in for it. One attractive girl in the Cold Weather can have the pick of twenty unattached males, and a lot of the other nineteen will be trying to stake a claim. Caprice was rather natural in the girl in such circumstances. Oh well, he thought, I'll just not let it go too far.

He decided to have a drink before changing, and walked down the aisle of rattan chairs overlooking the Cross Maidan. Mary and Margaret were already seated at a table. With a broad smile of welcome lighting her lovely face, Mary waved Walters over. He changed his course as if magnetized, sat down, and ordered a Tom Collins.

"Oh, Harry," said Mary,"I am so depressed about my tennis; either my eye is right out, or I am holding the racquet wrong."

"Well, if it's that," Walters replied before he could check himself, "I am right off my game myself, and I have fixed up with the Marker tomorrow to give me a few pointers. Why don't you come along?"

Mary didn't produce her diary and consult it. Instead she said: "What time?"

"Five thirty, right after I get away from the office."

"O.K., what's the Marker like?"

"Well, he's new, and not too booked up yet and very willing."

The aura of the English Rose began to suffuse Walters again. Margaret was, he thought decidedly plain, and the contrast made it worse. Mary wore a white cardigan over her tennis dress. She had, of course, been perspiring, and exuded a faint, but very agreeable, womanly odour, but flushed or sticky looking she was not; she glowed.

A rattling, as of drums, and sounds of a marching tune converged on the entrance of the Gymkhana. Walters glanced down the passageway and then at a slip of paper on the table.

"The 7th Baluchi Regiment," he remarked, and the girls turned round to see a cluster of servicemen filling the entrance with their bright coloured puggrees. They filed on to the maidan dressed in starched khaki tunics, wide stiff shorts, and puttees with green woollen tops, ready for the cocktail hour of bright musical entertainment. As the Band assembled, a very good looking, tall, slender young man with regular features and curly fair hair sauntered up to the table. Walters eyed him with, he realised, a feeling of defensive hostility. This was Roger Tufnell, generally regarded, including by himself, as something of a lady killer, besides which he was a man of means and son of the ex 'burra sahib' of the Bombay Trading Company which went back to the days of the British East India Company. Soon after his arrival two years ago, Roger had been followed by his new open Ford 10 car complete with dicky seat, a vehicle which was all too nicely adapted for partying.

Roger sat down, nodded to Walters, said hallo to Margaret, and beamed on the English Rose who asked him if he was coming to her party next week.

"Of course, I'll be there all right," said Roger.

"Oh yes, and you'll be coming, Harry, won't you?"

"Yes, I'm getting a reply off to your parents."

They conversed about the usual sort of goings on, and

the Races on Saturday at Mahaluxmi, Roger, pointedly, Walters thought, mentioning that he had a ticket for the Western India Turf Club enclosure. Then the Baluchis struck up and quietened the conversation as they all turned to watch. Walters ordered a round of drinks and signed the chit. He thought he'd better go and shower and change and hoped the girls would do the same, but he slipped Mary a note saying: "Can you come to dinner at the Yacht Club after tennis tomorrow?," and said cheerio.

The Baluchis had started off on their second half, parading the Band back and forth, and the evening crop of night-outers in dinner jackets and dresses was beginning to appear when Walters came out in a short-sleeved shirt and neatly arranged neckscarf. The table he had been at was empty. It was becoming dusk and he ordered a 'chota peg.' Flocks of flying foxes passed overhead on their regular evening flight path. Walters remembered how he had thought they were birds when he first saw them, and he always wondered where they were going. Then Lanky Newton appeared, and joined him in a drink before driving him home for an early meal.

At tennis the next day the English Rose was very friendly. Walters introduced her to the Marker, Esood Khan, a lithe muscular young man who said he was from Sialkot in the Punjab where his father manufactured tennis and squash racquets and hockey sticks. He turned Mary over to Esood and watched them discussing grips and shots. Evidently Mary's trouble was turning with her legs placed right, and as the Marker fired shots over to her and she started to do it correctly, adding grace to her movements, Walters couldn't take his eyes off her. "She's gorgeous," he said to himself.

They came off the court. "What's your trouble to-day?" Esood asked Walters.

"I don't know, timing I think, I'm just right off."

"Then we'll play a few games keeping the pace down and I'll watch you."

This seemed to work, and Walters found he was getting his eye in. "Right," said the Marker, "next four games we'll play all out."

Walters concentrated, and realising that Mary's eyes were on him, and here was a chance to show off, started to strike his best form and took both his service games besides nearly getting one of the Marker's in the course of some impressive rallies. Mary's approval was obvious. Walters felt sure things were going well for him there. He put the question he hadn't dared to ask sooner as soon as his bout was over.

"Will you be able to come on to the Yacht Club?"

"Oh, yes, I'm looking forward to it," Mary replied, "is it all right if Dad's driver picks me up at 10.30?"

"Of course," Walters tried to look matter of fact, but his face, dark and rather bony below bushy eyebrows, belied this as it split into a wide and toothy grin in which relief and excitement combined.

"I was hoping like anything you could make it," he said, "Do you have to go home first?"

"No, I've got my clothes here."

"Me too. Let's go and change now, and we can have a drink on the Yacht Club lawn if you are not tired of the Harbour."

"I'd love it," Mary said.

After lowering the net, the Marker came off the court smiling at his pupils. Walters paid him. "Salaam,

Esood," he said, "how about another session next week?"
He turned to Mary enquiringly. Her blue eyes sparkled
and she nodded.

"Same time then, Esood?"

The Marker noted it down. "O.K., salaams Mr Walters.
Salaams Missy Sahib."

Later, at a table close to the Harbour wall, they watched
the riding lights go up on the moored yachts, and the
fishing dhows coming home across the Bay, with
Elephanta Island going black in the sunset. Walters was
at peace, and his heart was full with this girl beside him.
A chill breeze crept in from the sea and they went in to
dinner: over all too soon, Walters thought.

He didn't fancy going to the Saturday Races any more
than he would have at any other time. He pictured
Roger Tufnell in tropical suit and topee, his badge
dangling from his lapel, dispensing charm, wit and
drinks in the Turf Club marquee; then put it from his
mind. Once you started getting jealous and competitive,
he told himself, you could be caught up for the whole of
the cold weather; with what at the end of it? All the
same, Mary did seem to be something very special.

This was the day he could use to go and look up the
Rishi after a swim with the chaps at Juhu, which was on
the way.

The Rishi was not that easy to find. The first two
people he asked in Thana village had no idea about his
whereabouts. The third, wishing to ingratiate, sent
Walters off on a completely wrong track. Eventually a
wallah selling pink drinks off a rusty trolley cart really
knew, and the Rishi's abode turned out to be three
quarters of the way to Lake Vehar on a hillside.

Walters came to a stone wall covered in cactus behind

which were several faded and tattered pennants on spindly sticks like those at a Buddhist shrine. Through an opening in the wall a weed-strewn cobbled path led to a weatherbeaten wooden door which evidently blocked a cave entrance. The door opened slowly, propelled by a skinny hand, as he approached, and just inside the Rishi sat on an upright but battered chair with a cane seat. Behind him the cave was small; parts of it were daubed with coloured paints, and in clefts were faded flower garlands, coloured plaster effigies and miscellaneous herbs and other items, including some liquids in bottles, all of which Walters took to be the standard tools of trade. The place had the sort of atmosphere he had looked forward to.

The Rishi put his hands and fingertips together pointing towards Walters, inclined his head and motioned him to a piece of bench opposite. Walters left his topee on, withdrawing the involuntary movement his hand had made to remove it. Speaking in cultured Hindi, the Rishi welcomed Walters with the vestige of a smile; "This morning I had a message of your coming," he said, "three years have passed for you in Hindustan and you are believing in the things of the spirit."

Walters tried not to look surprised, and said nothing.

"Speak to me of your needs," the Rishi continued.

"Your manner of the healing of the body and the soothing of the soul?" asked Walters.

The Rishi swept his arm round expressively, taking in the scrub jungle and palmetto palms going down to a sparkling corner of the lake where water buffalos, paddy birds on their backs, wallowed in the mud.

"Hindustan is a land of nature that never dies, never changes," he said. "It's Rulers, as will your Raj, come and go. Look into nature, seek out its ways and its meanings; apply them to yourself and to others you observe. You will never forget this land you call India; you will have troubles and sadness as well as joy; you will travel far, but you will live long enough and follow this path." The Rishi closed his eyes, his lips moving, while his free hand grasped some beads that were draped round his other arm.

Walters remained motionless. He was deeply impressed. He tried to hold the mood of the atmosphere, feeling that he had been taken seriously, and was rather flattered.

The Rishi opened his eyes and spoke again. "My powers come from the relinquishment of the body to higher thought, and hence the spirit emerges and guides the way, but when the body is stricken, nature supplies its remedies."

"If I am troubled I will come once more," Walters said, hoping this was the right way to break off.

"Ram Ram," the Rishi's hands went up and together again. Walters got up, eased his way through the door, and left.

"Really," he said, describing his encounter to Lanky that evening, "this chap I saw was no charlatan, Fakir or Witchdoctor. He was obviously well educated, and I felt that he could either put anyone in their place, or be of great help to them according to their genuine reasons. I just kept my mouth shut."

"For once!" Lanky winked. "Well, there you are, Harry. I wouldn't get too serious about it or shout it around, but you can read up something on it and have your fun."

The Cameron's special party for the English Rose was a big affair. There was a good sprinkling of the Services in mess kit and patrols, with the Navy predominating, and after them and their wives, a bunch of young people, of whom Walters recognised about half. The Camerons had done the best they could, but girls, naturally, were in short supply. In fact Walters collected only five out of twelve possible names on his dance engagement card, mainly because he and Bill Horley were nearly late due to the latter's car giving trouble. He had no doubt the English Rose was already heavily booked up.

When he had pushed through the crowd of Bearers ready to dispense the drinks, resplendent in their striped Regimental cummerbunds and puggree sashes, and into the Mess hall where dancing was starting, Walters saw Mary in the distance positively shining out of a long white strapless dress, with a wisp of organdie round her ivory shoulders, surrounded by beaux dominated by the fair head of Roger Tufnell. Walters felt glad he hadn't asked her to keep a dance for him in the circumstances.

When the supper interval came he managed to get near to Mary and, seeing him, she quickly came over. "What happened to you, Harry?" she asked, "I held out with a dance for you as long as I could."

"Awfully sorry," Walters replied, "but Bill's car conked out by Elphinstone Circle and we had to change a plug. "Anyhow, how are things going for you?"

"Well, I'm terribly spoiled and it's marvellous, but I feel rather tired and slightly sick, I don't know why."

"Too many parties!" Walters chided.

"No, Harry, I haven't been out since our second go of tennis day before yesterday. Last night I couldn't eat and went to bed early."

"Perhaps a touch of Bombay tummy: nothing worse I hope." Walters grabbed a plate of delicate little sandwiches and offered her one. "These look fairly harmless!"

"Thanks, Harry. Oh, there's my father signalling; I suppose he wants me to meet someone. I'll see you later on?"

She rustled off, her dress going in and out as she slid through gaps in the crowd.

The rest of the evening went quickly. Like Walters, there were plenty of men he knew who had half empty dance cards. It was the usual thing, and the drinks were varied and lavish, besides snacks and cigars. He didn't get near the English Rose again, and he and Bill Horley left straight after "God Save the King."

The next day over lunch in the Gymkhana, Walters heard that the English Rose had been taken ill and only just managed to see her party out. Capt. Gerry Cronshaw of the Indian Medical Service, one of three or four popular doctors who ministered to the European community, thought it was probably amoebic dysentery.

Two days later, Mary was in St. Elizabeth's Nursing Home on Malabar Hill, and when he could, Walters went to see her. One of the nuns told him he mustn't stay long, and a nurse showed him to Mary's room. She lay in bed, pale and devoid of make-up, looking awfully young to Walters, but still almost lighting up the pillows.

She gave him a wan smile as he pulled up a chair. "So you see it was something, Harry. I started with an excruciating pain just after talking to you at the party, and I knew it wasn't the sandwich!"

"What a shame: I'm so sorry this has happened and is going to spoil your Cold Weather," Walters said, "but the main thing is to get rid of it. Is there anything you need?" Filled with sudden emotion he took her hand in both of his.

The English Rose sighed and tightened her hand. "I can't eat a thing, and my head aches too much to read. It's all right, Harry, thank you, I think I'd like to sleep."

Walters stood up feeling rather futile. "I'm going on tour for ten days, Mary. When I come back I'll look in again if you are still here, and in any case we'll arrange something together. Just get well quickly!"

Mary nodded, forcing a smile. Walters crept out.

Walters remembered vividly the first time he went on tour, in fact to Ahmedabad as now, and he looked forward to it. He was very raw the first time, and he had never forgotten the sights and sounds of India up-country. Although no doubt different, it had all made him think of the Bible lands; the sheep and goats together and the village people in the chill of early morning, legs bare, but faces and heads all wrapped up; smells of dung fires and cooking, and then the bright day and the dust, always the dust. His company had a Branch in Ahmedabad now and things would be more regulated he supposed.

The Branch Manager met Walters at the Railway Station, and after an exchange of news and plans, Walters found himself in the Royal Hotel exactly where he had been last time, even possibly in the same room. In the morning he got out of the mosquito net and looked out on to the back compound of the hotel. The small banyan tree, the large peepul and two or three palms, behind which was lantana underbrush, were as Walters remembered them. Little striped palm squirrels churned up spurts of dust darting round for food, and groups of green parakeets with sharp pointed tails sped overhead screeching as they flew.

The Branch Manager had problems with his agents, and Walters set off with him to Baroda first, then Indore, and finally, Broach, which took them five days. The Branch Manager was anxious to get back as his wife was expecting a baby. He lacked a son, and many 'pujas' had to be done. This gave Walters a chance to relax and think. The usual reclining chairs, cane seated and long limbs extending in front at each side on which to rest the legs, were ideal. As soon as he could, Walters made for one of these on the Hotel verandah, and put a drink on the swing out bracket made handy for the purpose. He fell to thinking once more of what it could be like here in India with a wife to himself sharing all the adventures and amusing situations that cropped up. It would have to be someone strong, and, most of all, with a sense of humour. He thought of the English Rose and how someone like her might fit into his scheme of things. He began to see that health was indeed a serious matter, and also that there would have to be intermittent separations, especially when children arrived. It was one thing falling in love, but did the lives of the younger marrieds he now knew offer such an inviting future? No: he mustn't rush into anything if he could help it; the unwritten rules which Paul Wilson had outlined at that first social gathering were no doubt born out of the experience of others through the years. It was still more than a year before he could anticipate returning home. Perhaps he would then get a transfer to some other part of the world and this would all be behind him. Yet it would be a shame then to leave such memories unshared.

He reached for his empty glass and clapped his hands

loudly. A white clad 'Boy' appeared. "Dusra chota peg," said Walters. He remained as he was for nearly another hour. One thing was sure, he told himself; he wouldn't have the money to set up any sort of house on this contract, or maybe even the next. Perhaps he could save up. He would have to see, and he would have a serious discussion with Phil and Jean Renwick who had got married on Phil's first home leave last year. He allowed his thoughts to drift away from the problem, and settled down to enjoy the diminishing street sounds as the brief twilight fell, until mosquitos, attracted by the lights coming on in the verandah, drove him to his room to have a shower before dinner.

Back in Bombay's Victoria Station, Walters handed his bedding roll and suitcase to a coolie and threaded his way through the hundreds of families that seemed to spend their lives squatting on the platforms waiting for trains they might well never take. He took a taxi to Cumballa Hill.

The first of the others back after Walters was Bill Horley. After they had greeted each other, Bill immediately gave bad news of the English Rose.

"Mary Cameron is in rather a bad way from what I hear I'm sorry to say," he said. "Doc. Cronshaw is very worried that she may be getting an abscess on her liver according to the rumour. Anyhow he had her transferred to St. George's Hospital yesterday as her temperature refuses to come down and she can't take food. She must be awfully weak, poor girl."

Walters looked troubled. "I don't suppose it's easy for anyone to see her, is it?" he asked, without expecting Bill to know the answer.

"I shouldn't think so."

"Then I'll ring up Mrs Cameron tomorrow."

Mrs Cameron sounded almost in tears when Walters 'phoned. "Yes, Harry, she's very bad. Jim and I almost wish we hadn't let her come out now, and I want to get her home as soon as ever I can. I don't know how she could have caught dysentery so badly. It must have been in the Mess; one of the people in the kitchen perhaps, but no-one else has been affected."

Walters had been sympathetic and very worried; only her parents were allowed to see her at present, Mrs Cameron had added. He rounded off the report of his tour, got surrounded by all the work that accumulated in the office, and tried to carry on with his life as usual.

In the next few days the news got worse. They couldn't operate on Mary in her present condition, and yet she was not responding to the new sulpha drugs.

Walters decided at the weekend to go and see the Rishi.

The Rishi seemed glad to see Walters, and asked him to describe Mary and tell him all he knew about her, but particularly if he knew her birth date. To very many Hindoos their only proof of birth is a horoscope, something which the Rishi and others like him with some scholarly talents draw up for newly born village children, and use as a source of regular income. Luckily, remembering Mary's party, which had been some two weeks after her 19th birthday because it fell on the 24th December, Walters was able to give the right answer, but he naturally couldn't say at what time she had been born.

This seemed to provide the Rishi with something, and he consulted a sheaf of strange looking pictorial charts.

"It is indeed a dangerous time for your Missy Sahib

friend," he said, "the stars are bad. She was weak at birth and will have no brothers or sisters."

Walters realised that this was a fact, and waited for some hoped for advice.

"I will do some special 'puja'," the Rishi murmured, and taking down a bottle he put some liquid into a phial and gave it to Walters. "You must do some 'puja' according to your own religion," he said. "Tomorrow is your holy day, and If she drinks this the fever will go."

Walters salaamed and withdrew, grateful for anything, but thinking that the prospect of adminstering any medicine to the English Rose was just about impossible.

On Monday he again telephoned Mrs. Cameron who said that Mary had had a good night and they were going to see her at two o'clock, and perhaps Walters would like to come. Walters nervously agreed.

He stood in the background at the end of Mary's bed fingering the phial in his pocket. He could scarcely bear to look up, as he had taken in the sight of Mary's face on the pillow the moment he came in and been deeply shocked. Gone was the blush of her skin which now had a waxy pallor. Her jaw, no more rounded, looked clenched and tight and her cheeks sunken ; her blue eyes barely flickered under half closed lids. One hand, lying limply outside the sheet, looked transparent. Walters felt the colour rising in his face.

Mary opened her eyes a little and managed a faint smile at her parents who were speaking anxiously in the sort of platitudes reserved for the sick bed. Walters moved nearer, eyeing what seemed to be a glass of barley water on the bedside table. He turned his back to it hiding it. Mary gave him a look of what seemed to be recognition, and Walters, leaning forward, composed his face into what he hoped was a reassuring expression. At the same time he slid his hand with the open phial behind him and felt for the rim of the glass. The phial felt empty as he drew it back.

"We'd better go," said Mrs Cameron, "thank you for coming, Harry, Mary must have liked seeing another young person."

On his way home in the evening, remembering the Rishi's advice, Walters stopped at All Saints Church on Malabar Hill, and went in and said a prayer.

As the week went on Walters didn't have to telephone Mrs Cameron, and he didn't want to. The news got round that the English Rose was sinking and might not live. At the Hospital they could only wait and try to make her comfortable.

Walters now only felt like hiding himself, and tried to get buried in his work; but he began to be assailed by the most awful doubts, and his mind kept revolving round the possible outcome of such a serious situation at the Hospital.

Had he already gone too far in involving himself in things he yet knew so little about, and been mesmerised by the Rishi's aura of omniscience? Why hadn't he asked what the liquid was that he had been given? He had just assumed it was some standard herbal remedy for all too common diseases of the stomach and intestines. On the other hand some of these drugs came from poisonous plants, like digitalis. The English Rose had apparently rallied a bit on the Monday. Could he even have done something to hasten her death, and, in fact, be guilty of manslaughter at best? Or was it inevitable that the worst should come? He had never before been involved in such a knife-edge situation nor seen anyone so ill.

Yet, who was to say that the barley water by Mary's bedside had not remained untouched? Perhaps cleared away by some nurse as she slept.Walters' thoughts plagued him in the night as he tried futilely to put them in some sort of order. Desperately he tried to be optimistic. What about the Rishi's spiritual power? He was sure there were forces of good there which would not allow someone like Mary to be condemned. He must have faith.

The week dragged to an end. Then, on the Saturday morning an office colleague, a member of the Royal Indian Navy Reserve, came in and reported he had just heard Mary was a bit better.

By Monday no more news had gone round, and Walters plucked up the courage to 'phone Mrs Cameron.

"Yes," she said, and the relief in her voice was evident. "Mary's temperature has gone down a lot, and she has taken some broth. They think they can do some X-Rays if all goes well."

The English Rose was slowly recovering, but the doctors insisted that to avoid repercussions she must be on the first Mail boat to England as soon as her strength allowed it. It could only have been her youth that got her through the crisis was their opinion; Capt. Cronshaw admitted he had just about given up hope.

The day came, and Mrs Cameron helped Mary up the gangway as Walters stood below trying to keep his face from showing what he felt. He was thinking of the first time he saw Mary on the tennis court. The name he had given her then did not fit now; she was so thin, sallow and worn, looking as if she had come starving out of some awful jungle, her blue eyes staring. Could she ever get right again? He felt terrible.

Mary looked down. "Goodbye, Harry," she said, "and thank you for all you did for me; perhaps we'll have some tennis when you come home on leave next year. I'll write."

Walters wondered. "God bless you, Mary," he said, "get well soon." He felt depressed, almost bewildered, and he looked around to see if anyone else he knew was going aboard, but it was early in the season yet for 'home-leavers.'

He suddenly realised, as he walked away and made for his car, that he hadn't seen Roger Tufnell anywhere; in fact he had almost forgotten about him recently, for all that it mattered now. His spare thoughts had been mostly about his last visit to the Rishi. Of course he would have to go again very soon to the cave beyond Thana if only to find out whether the Rishi already knew the things that Walters would be recounting.

# ADVENTURE IN THE SACRED CITY.

In the ordinary way Harry Walters did not expect he would ever see the Sacred City of Benares, though he had really hoped to go there one day.

His fascination with the mysticism of India and the expression of spiritual truths within the Hindu religion, as well as its folklore, had kept its hold on him.

The chances to get away from Bombay for a few days leave were not that many, and located where it is, low lying on the approach to the Ganges delta, Benares did not seem the ideal place for a refreshing holiday break.

Then he was unexpectedly called upon to fill in for a couple of months in Calcutta where a fellow in the office there had gone on home leave.

"Harry," said his local manager, Peter Ormsby, "Head Office have asked me to help out while Ralph Jeffrey is away on his furlough. We are not exactly overstaffed here and I felt like protesting, but it is no good pretending that they would be in any way sympathetic."

It was already mid-April and Walters thought of the notorious Hot Weather in Calcutta, and the idea of landing up in some rather drab boarding house.

"You could stay in the Calcutta Light Horse Club," said Ormsby as if reading his thoughts. "Our Bombay Light Horse has reciprocity. I've been there myself and it's not at all bad. In Park Street, behind Chowringhee and only a couple of hundred yards from the Maidan. Pleasant garden too and within walking distance of the Office. Usually a good crowd of fellows there and a nice Mess."

Within a week Walters was on the evening train for the journey of two nights and a day. This passed off better than he expected as an Army friend of his joined him going as far as Jubbulpore, about half way. After that he settled down, conscious of not much more than the all–enveloping dust as the train sped on across flat and relatively featureless country.

It was the stops en route that provided the most diversion. Third class passengers came down from their perches half in and half out of the coaches as if they were overcoats being taken off pegs; to be replaced by others getting on. Somehow they all sorted themselves out without undue animosity.

Char and bidi wallahs, with urns of tea, rough rolled country cigarillos and suspect sweets, stridently proclaimed their wares along the station platforms. Beggars, maimed and otherwise, abounded, and railway track pi-dogs, many with one leg or part of it missing, fought as best they could for scraps.

Passengers with obscure bundles of possessions milled around or remained squatting or lying as if rooted to a small claim of territory.

Between times Harry Walters dozed fitfully and read.

The train finally puffed into Howrah Station and he got out and hailed the bearer who appeared from whatever part of the train he had been travelling in, packed up Walters' bedding roll and collected his suitcase.

Luckily a good friend of Walters, Tony Weaver, not long since transferred from Bombay, was on the platform to meet him.

"Well, hello, Tony," he said. "Good of you to come here at this early hour."

"Nice to see you, Harry," Tony said. "Who'd have thought you'd be coming over here. Anyhow I've got my car and brought my bearer too as I heard you'd booked into the Light Horse Club. He can show your chap just how to get there with your stuff while we go to my place for breakfast."

They drove from Howrah over the bridge across the Hoogly river into Calcutta proper, and Walters was struck by the great size of the city and also how European it looked, and clean too, compared to Bombay. In places it reminded him of Marseilles, and parts of London. Except, of course, for the awful sticky heat and the difference in its denizens.

As the days went by the air grew hotter and hotter and the humidity level rose, seeming even more than it was in a temperature of 100 degrees plus.

The company at the Club was good as Ormsby had predicted, and Calcutta full of interest, but with his goal of Benares in his sights, Walters was glad to find himself on the train once more heading for Bombay.

His first leg took him to the junction of Moghal Sarai by early morning, and leaving most of his baggage at the station, he took off on a branch line, after a wait of no more than an hour, for the Sacred City on the Ganges and beloved of Shiva.

His bearer, Sana, was equally excited and as full of anticipation as Walters. The train rattled in over the iron bridge spanning high above the river Ganges itself and stopped beyond the centre of the city where the ground levelled off and stretched towards the cantonment. They got off and found a tonga to take them to Clark's Hotel. Once installed Walters sent Sana off knowing how much it meant to him to be able to immerse himself in 'Gangaji.'

After he had finished a lunch of the most he could eat in the searing heat of the day, an evil–looking character tidily dressed but with an ingratiating manner and shifty eyes, came up to Walters and salaaming, handed him a grubby card which read:–

'Haran Ch. Moitra, Travelling and Social Guide,
Benares Cantt. Benglow 94/46, Cantt.'

Walters hesitated. The man spoke in English.

"I am experienced local guide, sahib. Many sahibs are having confidence in me."

And from a pocket hidden down the side of his long shirt he produced a sheaf of 'Chittis' extolling his virtues. Walters glanced at a couple of them; they seemed genuine enough. He decided to check at the hotel desk.

"Yes, sahib," said the clerk in the somewhat makeshift office behind. "It is important to have a guide in the holy centre of the City. As well as pilgrims there are many bad people."

Clark's Hotel was on the edge of the Cantonment. Walters set off in a tonga with the guide Moitra, by–passing the city centre and arriving on the river bank to the side of the Ghats.

"We shall hire a boat from this man, sahib," Moitra said, indicating one of several boatmen clustered around a small rough wooden landing–stage about which their boats were drawn up on the muddy bank. They looked substantial enough.

Moitra gave an exhibition of difficult haggling. "Four Rupees for one hour, sahib," he said. "From the river all the ghats can be seen and good for photographs. They cannot be reached by themselves." Walters paid up.

They set off slowly upstream. The current was sluggish

but the water, to his surprise, looked very blue and quite clean. Various undefinable objects floated by; then Walters jumped to see half a dozen men, overboard from their boat, swimming around a dead bull which they were evidently towing out to leave in midstream, watched by a line of vultures along the barren far side bank of the wide river, ready to set on anything drifting ashore.

Moitra took in Walters' gaze. "Those vultures succeed to keep the river and bathing places clean here, sahib; also the gharials. Look, there is one of those there!"

Walters saw the narrow, almost swordfish–like snout of the creature break the water and close on a floating object.

"But is there not a big risk of epidemics?" Walters asked.

"No sahib, the Ganga flows down from Benares and before a mile has passed nothing bad remains. People who have died from disease are taken to that far bank and all burnt."

The ghats of the City are stepped terraces down to the river where, Walters learned, the greater part of the foreshore is taken up with the private bathing establishments of rajahs and land–owners, and the imposing dwellings in which they stay with their retainers and hangers–on when they come to purify themselves.

Moitra had been right to take Walters out in the boat. A panoramic view of the nearside waterfront was exposed to his eyes, such as never could have been taken in from the City bank. He began to think Moitra was a good investment.

"After the landlords and rajahs, sahib," Moitra

explained, "ghats are owned by temples and their holy men, then by richer people and purdah ladies. The remaining areas are public for anybody" – like Sana, Walters thought – "who can find their way here."

As the boatman paddled nearer and held his oars against the current, it was easy to see the public bathing ghats. Masses of people were splashing and ducking under, almost fully clad. Then they gave way to others and picked up odd pieces of clothing and cloth that passed for towels. The burning afternoon sun on dhotis and saris held in the wind completed the drying operation.

Walters was somewhat surprised to hear that there was only one burning ghat. They drifted a short way downstream to look at it.

"No Europeans can approach it on land," Moitra said, "Burning bodies goes on all day."

Walters saw the whole process beginning with the remnants of a burnt body being flung into the river.

Up above three or four pyres were burning, and higher still corpses bedecked with flowers were brought in shoulder high on rough stretchers. Numbers of cows could be seen as if they were looking on.

"The bodies wrapped in white are men," Moitra said, pointing, "and those in red are of women. The men carrying them are relatives. No women are allowed to be up there."

Walters watched the progress of a new arrival, a man. The corpse was precariously carried down to the water's edge where the head was uncovered, and one of the men poured handfuls of water over the face. Then the corpse seemed to get left almost half in and half out of the water while the relatives mounted the steps.

"What are they doing now?" he asked Moitra.

"They go to buy wood, sahib, very expensive. Merchants are selling it up there at the entrance to the ghats."

Sure enough, the relatives of the body in white returned and, finding a space swept clear by untouchables, started to build a pyre, laying the wood crosswise, then bringing up the corpse and placing it on top until a priest appeared, evidently to do an incantation, and removed what flowers remained for the nearby cows, some of which had already helped themselves, to consume.

More wood was laid across the body; then a man stepped forward and set fire to the pyre with sheaves of straw.

"That is the nearest relative, sahib," Moitra said. "The others are going away now, and will fast for 10 days and he will follow them."

Walters had seen the end of an earlier burning. The nearest relative had waited until the fire burned down; he then removed the human remains with a wooden prong and threw it in the river.

As the boat turned to regain the landing place the body of a small child floated by. Walters shuddered and pointed to it.

"Oh yes, sahib," Moitra explained, "children up to six years of age are not burned, but tied with a stone and thrown into the river. That one has broken away."

All very practical, Walters thought, but not pretty. Despite the stench rising from the old moat bordering the City walls, and the jostling pilgrims, he was glad to get away from the hotch-potch waterfront and into the crooked bazaar streets.

He went with Moitra as far as the Golden Temple with its twin domes of thick gold leaf and floors with inlaid silver pieces. They took in the Temple of the Cow next door and lingered shoeless just over the thresholds of both, beyond which devotions were in full swing. The air was full of incense, flowers and the noise of cymbal and drum.

Baleful looks were shot at the European infidel before they withdrew. With a knowing leer Moitra, as a grand finale, led Walters away to the Nepali Temple of Shiva dedicated to newly weds, and no female foreign tourists allowed. The picturisations in carving were frank in the extreme, enough Walters thought, for the lovers to find space away from their undivided family to be able to exercise the suggestions of the gods.

The heat was great. Walters hailed a tonga and dismissed Moitra at the hotel with a sizeable tip; he had done an excellent job. "After sundown I will go back and look around by myself," he said.

Moitra looked doubtful. "Sahib, you must be careful and not go into streets too dark and narrow."

Walters, fired by the atmosphere about the main temples, said that he would not, and only waited until the worst heat of the day subsided with the sun. He went to the desk and asked the clerk to arrange for his bearer, Sana, when he returned, to be told where his master had gone.

The tonga dropped him as near as it could penetrate to the Golden Temple. Immediately he felt a change in the air. Mostly because of the gathering dusk, Walters reckoned, and the fact that many sources of light were taking over the illumination. Overhead street lights merged into the gloom above, their duties at ground level being taken over by shadeless electric bulbs of many colours, or acetylene lamps in building recesses where goods were being sold, and men were squatting, working endlessly on a variety of hand industries.

Elsewhere flames guttered from naked oil lamps and candles at the entrances to holy places and within, casting shadows in different directions according to the draughts of the fetid air hanging heavily before the night wind might come.

Walters was dressed inconspicuously, without his topee and sun-tanned, hoping thus to disguise his alien origin. Despite this, several passers-by looked at him in a way that he hoped was prompted more by curiosity than hostility. He stopped walking and found a vantage point to look at the passing scene. Instinctively he placed himself with his back against a wall where it formed a shallow alcove.

From here he could take in all the turmoil, noise and colour as more people emerged from the surrounding narrow streets and made for the temples, momentarily blending with the devotees coming out. Pilgrims for the most part by the offerings and flowers they were bearing.

True holy men or priestly charlatans were enveloped by the throng, mutely mingling with, or openly importuning, its members. A bearded guru with a small retinue of 'Chelas,' or youthful acolytes, steered them aside; then paused to put a coin in the half–coconut extended by an emaciated ascetic.

Round the steps of the temples, fakirs, fat and thin, bedaubed liberally with ash, sat motionless, one with a shrivelled arm held eternally on high.

Walters ceased to note the passage of time. He sensed a hypnotic numbness of his mind and a strange inner warmth.

He moved away, pushing through where the crowd was thinnest, and wandered, not noting where he was going, curious to see what lay around the next corner. He became aware at one point that three youths had fallen in behind him; then, at the entrance to a narrow alleyway, one of them jostled him.

Seeing bright lights he turned into the alley and found himself looking into the many coloured interior of a large shrine to one side. The image within, bluish of skin, he knew to be that of Krishna. The lights shone out on his face showing clearly who he was, and the leading youth hissed, "Death to the feringi."

Walters froze, but, seeing no weapon brandished, bent down in a gesture of removing his shoes; then he turned and found the youths had melted away. He was fully alert now, and ready to admit that he could not be an acceptable part of the religious fervour pervading this place of pilgrimage.

He remembered what Moitra had said, and decided to wait before retracing his steps. He took in his situation for the first time wondering what had directed him here. The shrine was in the side wall of a dead end, sealed ahead of him by a heavy iron–studded door with a small iron grill through which wafted fresher air, and what seemed to be the dim light of a rising moon. He grasped the heavy door handle and forced it open. It was a small room like a dungeon, and a larger grill on the far wall faced him with a shaft of moonlight cutting the floor. On the left wall was a plain door.

Walters let go of the entrance door which clanged to, and adjusted his eyes to the partial gloom, only to find in horror that there was no sign of any handle on the inside of the door. With a dry mouth he made for the side door.

Another room, smaller, but well lit by two large wax candles, revealed itself. Between the candles, on a wooden dais, his copious white beard extending to his crossed legs, sat a corpulent elderly saddhu. On his forehead was the trident-like scarlet mark of Krishna.

Walters felt the tension going out of him as his breathing returned to normal. Evidently this was the keeper of the shrine outside. The man hardly stirred, but his downcast eyes rose and took in his unusual visitor. Walters stayed where he was, knowing that he had not been trapped.

He pulled himself together and took on an attitude, respectful and apologetic at which the holy man smiled and beckoned to him. He spoke in recognisable English.

"My son," he said. "You have strayed dangerously but the Lord Krishna has guided your footsteps here where you received His protection. None but Hindus should venture alone at night where the streets are dark and narrow for fear of committing sacrilege.

"You are coming to Benares" – the priest looked younger as he rose to his feet – "seeking for the truth, but now you must hurry back. Come."

The holy man took an L-shaped iron bar from a niche and led Walters to the outer door, and sliding the bar into a small socket, opened it.

The sound of pealing bells penetrated the alley. "Follow that sound," the priest said. "You will come to the temple of the Lord Krishna and see his golden image. Not far on to the right are the golden domes of Shiva. Your friends have come to look for you and are there."

Walters bowed, saluted in deep gratitude, and trustingly followed the directions, realising that he had wandered in circles.

Distinguishable on the edge of the throng of the pious and impious was Moitra, and behind him in his black cap, his white garments clear in the moonlight, was Sana, his bearer.

# THE AMOROUS TAPEWORM

Her name was Anita Temple and she was Gilbert Morton's burra memsahib. When Gilbert arrived in Bombay in 1934 she was probably about 35 years old.

Her husband of ten years, Forbes, was an amiable, easy going man five years her senior. He had to be the way he was.

Back in 1921, when a Royal personage visited India and stayed at Government House in Bombay for a few days, at the Ball in his honour he twice danced with Anita Temple as she later was. She must have been a beautiful and alluring young woman then, a slender and willowy charmer with a complexion yet unsullied by the tropical climate.

The attention she received from the distinguished visitor advanced her social and sexual desirability enormously. It also made her very personally aware of what she might call her magnetism.

This was enough for a few years to make her very 'persona grata' at GH with the Governor, and as she played a nice game of tennis HE was glad to have her at his afternoon parties. His ADCs found no fault in this, and Forbes was happy enough to be an indulgent onlooker. Anita was in her element.

The trouble with life in the tropics is that weather, food and disease, in reverse order really, take their toll, and the effects are more dire on women in general than on men.

Oddly enough, timely child bearing can sometimes help the female system, and is said to be easier in hot humid climates. Anita and Forbes had not been able to have children, an anomaly which sometimes affects highly sexed women.

This fact enabled Anita freely to exercise the reputation she had gained as a man killer, and then, although she caught only a fairly mild case of jaundice, it caused her to lose nearly two stone in weight, which obstinately refused to come back.

Now it is a fact that even Europeans in India fall victim to tapeworm, a horrible parasite which, while it can be got rid of, is not always immediately suspected and diagnosed until, rendering nutrition almost ineffective, a victim becomes distressingly thin.

Europeans in far distant countries cling to the habits and diet they have been used to at home. Raw, insufficiently cooked meat, like a rare steak or, much more often, undercooked pork, is taken to be the offender when it comes to tapeworm.

Though having become outwardly almost scrawny in body, and with the beauty of her face etched over in lines, inwardly Anita had lost none of her conviction that she was sexually alive, and none of her anxiety to prove it.

It is something of an enigma with many women whether they delude themselves into refusing to accept that the artifice of their good looks can be losing its power, or if, because they know what results they want to get, they are actually quite unaware of their lack of effective physical assets. Possibly they do not fully use a long mirror.

For whatever reason, on account of her behaviour, Anita Temple had become a figure of some ridicule at best, or even a distinct embarrassment to those, mainly male, who found themselves in her path.

Accordingly – probably some waggish memsahib had coined it – starting in the mahjong and bridge morning sessions, Anita was referred to as: 'The Amorous Tapeworm,' and the name stayed with her.

Within a couple of weeks of his arrival, Gilbert Morton received a chit at the office from Anita Temple asking him if he would like to come round and have dinner and spend the evening at her bungalow. Also, would he ask that nice boy Nigel Bardolf who was in his chummery.

Gilbert was a bit surprised. He had only met his boss's wife on one occasion so far, and the other thing was that Forbes Temple was away up-country for a week; however, he supposed it was nothing out of the ordinary, a sort of gesture of hospitality in fact.

He showed the message to Nigel when he got back in the evening. Nigel, in fact, had come out on the same boat so was just as raw as Gilbert.

"What do you think of it, Nigel?" he asked.

"Well, it might be rather pleasant; I'll come along and chaperon you. Is she nice?"

"I've only met her once," Gilbert replied. "She must have been rather good-looking originally, but she's getting on a bit now, and painfully thin. Right, if you are on, I'll 'phone her from the office in the morning and fix when; dinner jackets no doubt."

Gilbert and Nigel presented themselves at the Temples' bungalow precisely at 8 pm two days later and were ushered in by an impressive looking bearer.

Anita Temple rose from a sofa in the lounge and greeted them warmly.

"Introduce me to your friend."

"Ah, yes," Gilbert said, "this is who you asked me to

bring if I could, Nigel Bardolf."

"Glad you could come, and to meet you," Anita said with a flashing smile.

A moment later a tall and slender woman of about thirty with well groomed shoulder length straight blonde hair appeared through the doorway from some other room.

"Ah, the other member of our foursome," Anita said. "Bobby, you've heard about the newest addition to Forbes' staff, Gilbert Morton. Gilbert, Roberta Bowen."

"How d'you do," Gilbert said, stepping forward and shaking hands.

"And Bobby, meet Nigel Bardolf who's in Gilbert's chummery here in Pali Hill."

The bearer came in with a full ice bucket and put it down on a tray of drinks.

Gilbert had not got quite used to drinking whisky with a full glass of soda and ice cubes, the classic 'Chota peg,' but it was refreshing on a hot evening.

Nigel hesitated when he saw the women preparing 'White Ladies,' and then decided he would join them in one.

They talked about the good sense, or good fortune, of arriving in India to catch the beginning of the Cold Weather.

As far as Gilbert and Nigel were concerned the evenings seemed just not uncomfortably warm, and they were glad to hear the bearer busy with a Flit gun on the verandah and then proceeding to lay the dinner table there.

It turned out that Roberta's husband, Dudley Bowen, in the Advertising business, was also away, on a visit to Karachi. "He's got a branch of his firm there," Bobby said, "also in Lahore. The Calcutta office does south east India."

"What are you in, Nigel?" she asked.

"Cox and Kings."

"Oh really," Anita joined in. "You've come in because Dick Spencer's gone off to take over Rawalpindi, I suppose. We knew him pretty well."

A little background music from the radiogram accompanied some more drinks. Anita began to sparkle ominously.

The bearer appeared in the opening to the verandah. "Khana tiyar hai, memsahib." He announced to Anita. Dinner was ready.

The meal consisted of mulligatawny soup, a mutton curry embellished by all the trimmings in variety and number that neither Gilbert or Nigel had seen before, and a delicious sweet called noka cream. The men drank McEwans lager and both women imbibed red wine fairly liberally.

The women were talking about servants when Gilbert and Nigel rejoined them for coffee and Cointreau.

"Our hamal, Laloo, has been with us for five years now," Roberta was saying. "One thing, you do feel safe out here when you are left on your own, don't you? Laloo sleeps across my bedroom doorway while Dudley's away."

"I know, so does our chap," said Anita, "and patrols the verandah as well ostensibly. Main thing is the way these people can manage to pass the night sleeping on the thinnest of bedrolls, if you could call them that, quite happily."

Gilbert knew about hamals by now; they had one in the chummery. The hamal did all the work around the house that it was beneath a bearer to do; cleaning, dusting, polishing, lighting, locking up and so on, and getting hold of the sweeper and the dhobi when required.

The radiogram was turned on to dance music, lights lowered and rugs kicked aside.

"Come on, let's dance," Anita, a little unsteady, said, clasping Gilbert.

The music, a blues, was no doubt intentionally languid. Bobby and Nigel moved comparatively decorously. Anita steadied herself against Gilbert then moved smoothly, holding him in an embrace which, from a better covered woman, would be voluptuous. As it was her knees were hard and bony enough to keep Gilbert clear of any latent desire.

Anita did not seem to notice this, but broke off, simpering, after another record was over.

"Well, I am your burra sahib's wife," she said, "I mustn't lead you astray, but you do dance nicely. Let's have a Martini."

Bobby was looking at Anita a little bit protectively and with just a touch of apprehension, Gilbert thought, after they had changed partners and he, avoiding Nigel's eye, noticed that he was getting the treatment rather more intensely than he had himself.

In the intervals Anita, predictably, turned the conversation to female friendships, asking Gilbert and Nigel what girls they had left behind them.

"Not many unattached girls out here," she said. "There will be some from home as usual, out for the season and sometimes for a husband, but spoiled and expensive. You are too young and underpaid for that." Then, archly, "You'll have to make the best of hags like us!"

Roberta winced. She clearly decided the evening was better over.

"Time for me to go," she said. "I live more or less on the way to your chummery; will you boys see me home?"

Gilbert looked for Anita's reaction to this. It was not bad, and her response was unchallenging.

"Oh, come on Bobby, not yet surely," she said.

"Darling, you have forgotten that I am hunting tomorrow morning."

"Oh yes, of course. Oh well, I suppose I am a bit tired." Anita yawned delicately.

Back at the chummery, Gilbert and Nigel, more intrigued than relieved, reviewed the experience.

"What do you make of it?" Gilbert asked.

"Amazing," said Nigel. "How many Europeans in your office?"

"Four, and I'm the only one not married."

"I don't think I envy you your boss's wife, but surely she will be more discreet than tonight in the ordinary way and in the Temples' own circle, not to mention those like you in the office?"

"Yes, I suppose we are new young blood fresh out from home," said Gilbert. "We must have been something of a coup for them this evening. Lucky for us, perhaps, that Anita had too much to drink."

It is a fact that people like Anita Temple are regarded indulgently with some pity and almost affection by those whose path they do not cross, but to become embroiled with them and provide fuel to the fire of idle gossip is dangerous.

It was only a matter of days after Gilbert and Nigel's evening out that they knew they had survived a brush with the Amorous Tapeworm.

Others had not been so lucky, Gilbert heard. There was the case a year before of Colin Crosthwaite who had had the misfortune to work in Barclays Bank where the Temples had their account.

Young men who were sent out to India by their employers were hand-picked. Firstly to be a credit to their firms, and secondly so that they should not be out of place themselves in a narrow and class conscious society.

This good start, Gilbert found, had its social obligations, which, since he filled the bill, he did not find it hard to keep. Apart from reasonably good behaviour in public and respectable attire, the main thing was to keep away from unsuitable personal entanglements.

Consorting privately with Eurasian girls, Anglo-Indians as known, even if probably country-born of European stock, many of whom were undeniably attractive and willing, was frowned on, but not condemned out of hand if the involvement was not advertised, but if it led to the possibility of marriage, a quick return home for the young man was the likely prescription.

Covert visits to the brothels in Grant Road were acknowledged, at the visitor's risk, which was considerable and not worth a second try.

Falling into the trap of the Amorous Tapeworm was not in the same category exactly, but sufficient to show up the victim's stupidity and lack of self-control.

Crosthwaite was ideal bait for Anita Temple, being anxious to oblige his Bank's customers and somewhat naive.

Anita lavished all her fading charm on him during visits to the Bank, picking on insignificant financial matters to be ushered into his side office.

In places such as the Gymkhana, the Yacht Club or the Taj Mahal Hotel, and particularly on visits to the ever popular Cinema, she got to pawing Colin and kissing him in public.

Her ultimate objective was the Temples' weekend shack on Juhu Beach. These shacks, backed by coconut groves, dotted the rising banks of sand and coarse grass well above the shoreline. Many were well shaded, and some substantial enough for a comfortable weekend stay with better than camping facilities. Others, like the Temples', were roofed and framed entirely with palm fronds, and apart from a few sticks of furniture and 'palangs' – beds strung with strong cord or thongs – depended on what could be brought out by car on any particular occasion.

Husbands with wives anything like Anita as a rule order their own lives in one of several ways. Either they divorce them, hang on to them for sheer convenience while finding solace in someone else's arms, or condone what they see as merely a kind of eccentricity, and pursue separate interests within their own circles.

Forbes Temple came within the third category. He was a yachtsman and seldom missed a regatta or other event at the Yacht Club which, of necessity, took place at weekends. Furthermore, he shared a boat with an equally keen friend, Sam Jarvis. As regards Anita, Forbes had never quite got over why she married him, and ever since her days as a spoiled and noted beauty, he indulged her whims and ignored her faults, seeming to be unaware of the reputation she had acquired. At cocktail parties Forbes gravitated towards the sailing set, leaving Anita to flit animatedly from group to group in the manner of a humming bird in a flower garden.

As a wife, apart from the inordinate amount of time she spent on herself, from the neck up, before a mirror, Forbes had little to complain of about Anita in her role of housewife and memsahib. People seldom refused an invitation to the Temples' parties whether for one reason or another.

To say that Anita Temple had entirely lost her charm and persuasiveness would not be true. Her vivacity and lithe movements were infectious, and her almost innocent way of first gaining a man's attention was disarmingly misleading.

Colin Crosthwaite was unsubtle and not a lady's man. He went down well with everyone at the Gymkhana Club, swam at Breach Candy baths, played tennis, cricket, squash, and rugby football in the monsoon, and was as solid in appearance as Anita was frail. Ironically, absorbed in his sporting activities, he was not as much concerned by the lack of female company as most others who made up the large number of single men out in India on their first contract.

But, as Gilbert's informant told him, Colin saw Anita at the Bank once a week at least and was soon never absent from the Temples' parties. It was also natural that he enjoyed swimming and surfing at Juhu on Sundays, an activity that Anita was not slow to notice.

She was not all that keen on lounging around at Juhu where the Temples' shack was one of the small flimsier ones. Then people owning others nearby noticed that it had been reinforced, had a new padlock and hasp, and a few more inside comforts such as coir mattresses and floor mats.

Neighbours are always curious, and when Anita was seen more often, and clad in a bathing costume which, while softening the more angular parts of her, showed also that she had not completely lost some of her curves, they linked it with the presence of the burly figure of Colin Crosthwaite.

Like a spider with a succulent bluebottle, the Amorous Tapeworm had a new morsel in her clutches. Rumour had it from sounds within the shack on more than one balmy Sunday afternoon in January that Anita was climbing with enthusiasm all over the compliant body of young Crosthwaite.

Situations like this, if continued unchecked, can lull the participants into a false sense of security. The demeanour of Anita Forbes on her frequent visits to Barclays Bank was now unmistakable to Colin's seniors who viewed it with mounting concern.

Visitors to the Temples' were accustomed to the sort of entertainment provided unconsciously by Anita, but now that her attention was concentrated on one particular individual they began to feel worried and head Colin off into different groups when they could.

Gilbert related all that he had been told of the Crosthwaite affair to Nigel.

"I suppose it was not possible to tell Colin to lay off?" Nigel asked.

"Well, not impossible I imagine, but certainly difficult," Gilbert said. "Anita would have taken it out on him, or Forbes, or someone, tactlessly, at that stage."

"Forbes, of course, is my burra sahib, a sound businessman, and no fool. He was bound to react sometime."

"So what happened next?" Nigel enquired.

"Well, it wasn't long," said Gilbert, continuing the story, "before Anita decided to make a weekend of it at Juhu."

"The annual Regatta at the Yacht Club took in a whole Saturday and Sunday, and Forbes, Sam Jarvis, and others always stayed in the Yacht Club chambers overnight.

Out at Juhu, that Saturday evening was perfect enough, with the moon on the water, to turn anyone's head.

"Have you ever woken up here in the early morning and seen the fishing dhows coming home with the rising sun on their lateen sails? 'Let's do it,' is the sort of thing Anita might have said to Colin Crosthwaite.

"And she invited him out to dinner.

"There are two places providing good meals at Juhu. The Juhu Country Club run by a European, Mrs. Richards, and much less pretentious than its name, comprising a tea garden, inside dining room and half a dozen bedrooms; and Jeejeebhoy's providing food and drink only.

"Jeejeebhoy, a venerable Parsee, is apparently a stickler for etiquette and proper attire, and an upholder of beach morals.

"Anita and Colin accordingly went to the Country Club about a quarter of a mile along the sandy beach from the shack, had a good meal with plenty of drink and returned to the shack with a bottle of water for breakfast tea.

"The seriousness of an afternoon frolic at Juhu might be exaggerated by tongues ready to wag at anything, but an all night liaison is another thing, and even hurricane lamps show a dappled light through palm matting.

"Forbes Temple had had enough. During the next week he held a careful discussion with his opposite number at Barclays Bank, and not very long afterwards Colin Crosthwaite was on a boat home."

"Well," said Nigel, "I think I have a more discriminating attitude towards women, but I am glad that we have been put on guard. I imagine that you are close enough for safety. I mean that even the Amorous Tapeworm must by now stop short of shitting on her own doorstep!"

According to Anita Temple, young Crostwhaite, now that he was out of the way, had made a great play for her, and while the sympathies of Bombay society were with the young man, Forbes, feeling less need of his wife's bedroom accomplishments than running a good business and sailing round Elephanta Island, wisely put the matter behind him.

Bombay comes completely alive in the short cold weather season with every kind of diversion. Winter palaces and mansions are opened up, filled with princely owners, their families and guests, and surrounded by servants in gaudy livery. The lawns of the Western India Turf Club where the Governor and his entourage holds court are even more colourful than Ascot. Also at Mahalaxmi are Horse Shows and Polo.

Young bachelors as newly out as Gilbert and Nigel are in some demand by people playing host to pretty debutantes from Britain to join private parties, even though their funds cannot extend to taking things further on their own with any fresh young beauty they may have met.

Whatever the pastime, in the line of sport or otherwise, there were plenty of other young chaps to join in with. The affair of the Amorous Tapeworm faded into the background.

Friday or Saturday night at the Taj Mahal Hotel became the place to be.

After a four of tennis at the Gymkhana and changing there into the essential dinner jacket, Gilbert, Nigel and others, unless they had an invitation to dinner somewhere, usually started the evening off by going to the Hotel's Harbour Bar, with Mabel Hodgkins or some other entertainer at the piano.

The first time this happened, a chap in Gilbert's office, Alec Smith, whose wife was due back from England on the next mailboat, joined them and suggested a meal at Green's Hotel just round the corner, and doing the 10 pm show at the Eros Cinema.

When they emerged from Green's, the pavement was already covered with sleeping male bodies. Gilbert, a few drinks inside him, started to shoulder others, still pedestrian, out of the way. He felt ashamed and affronted that such a congested mass of humanity should actually be lying in their path and shoved some of these aside with his foot. Alec bridled at this.

"Don't do that, Gil," he said. "You'll have to get used to it, it's perfectly normal, just step over them. They are not necessarily vagrants."

Revulsion welled up in Gilbert. "But where in hell do they come from?"

"Out of any of these back street hovels," Alec said, indicating grubby doors, some obviously leading down to cellars. "You'll notice that there are no women or children. Those poor beggars have to sweat it out in the sweltering darkness throughout the night, hoping for a suggestion of sea breeze."

"God, no wonder there is such mortality," Nigel said. "How awful!"

"To keep your reason in India," Alec went on as they crossed the wide road in front of the imposing arch of the 'Gateway of India,' "it is no good trying to be indignant about what goes on around you, much less have it prey on your sympathies. It will never change."

"I have found it hard to imagine where all these people come from, at all hours of the day or night," Nigel said. "I know they breed like flies, of course."

"Calcutta is worse," Alec said. "There is hope of money in the cities, and water, and food of a sort, and no drought or famines. That is the draw. They simply squat or live with relatives in the 'Chawls' – the workers tenements you pass when you go down to the office. One day, when you have a car, drive through Bombay's shanty suburb of Sion, it is indescribable."

Gilbert Morton, as the weeks passed, found that he was able to come to terms with the divisions in Indian society; the unbridgeable gulf between rich and poor, caste and caste. Life would indeed be impossible otherwise as Alec Smith had said. It was a sort of apprenticeship for Europeans.

Indians, high born or wealthy, or both, showed the way and the customs to those from Britain who came to rule or trade or preach. The first category reluctantly, yet diplomatically, fell in with the system, content to reform it by uncontroversial means. The preachers did little better than to foment injustices and fan discontent. Stony ground for them.

Rioting, except communal, Hindu against Moslem, appeared to be almost non-existent such is the effect of the system of caste where people accept their lot in life, when it is poverty, as something handed out to them by fate, and capable of improvement by their present actions only when they return to earth in the next life.

It was now well into the cold weather, but the social season had not passed its peak. The dry, starry nights were softened with the precipitation of an early dew. Coming out of the ballroom into the grounds of Government House, seats and tables bore heavy beads of moisture which the caparisoned servants were diligently mopping off. Evening tailcoats and ballroom gowns brushed against the wet leaves of bushes sparkling in the coloured lights.

That had been a week ago on Gilbert Morton's second invitation to G.H., not normal, some ADC had evidently made a mistake.

Gilbert knew a few girls by then to get his dance card half full; it was all he wanted. It gave him more time to sample the food and drink, smoke a leisurely cigar with the crest on it's band, and look at the striking variety of the guests. In between, he spoke to a few fellows he knew, and several memsahibs, among them the Amorous Tapeworm.

He thought that Anita looked rather chastened, almost lost. Could she still be seeing herself as she once was, providing the competition, though now reluctant to face it?

In and out of light and shadow, dresses, saris, uniforms and regalia flowed like multi-coloured rivulets; jewellery and gold and silver sari borders flashing as would sunlight on the ripples.

At the Taj Mahal Hotel on Saturday nights parties from the Native States were still coming, and here, the details of the princess's clothes could be seen at close quarters.

Gilbert, Nigel and others did not need the stimulus of female company on these occasions. It was like watching a lavish stage show from the front stalls. Gilbert marvelled particularly at the pretty little Royal ladies from Nepal. Like exotically dressed dolls they were, their greyish tan complexions as flawless as Dresden china.

One evening when Gilbert had been out to a dinner party with Alec Smith and his newly returned wife, Angela, Nigel arrived back late, and in a state of some agitation.

"Christ, Gil," he spluttered. "The worst happened at the Taj tonight. I got into the clutches of Anita Temple. She and Forbes and the Bowens were at a table across the dance floor, and she spotted me on my way back from the toilet after I had carefully circled round to get there. She got up and asked me to join them, and I was caught."

"Well, Forbes was there, wasn't he?" Gilbert said.

"Yes, but wait. The Tapeworm had had a few drinks as usual, and how I hate dancing with that woman. This time she nearly castrated me! No good you laughing. You've got immunity."

Gilbert wiped the grin off his face. "Was there anyone we know well at the Taj?" he asked.

"Several, apart from the two chaps I was with, and of course, I was relying on old Monty Martin for a lift home. So what does the Tapeworm do but send Forbes off with the Bowens, saying that she must show the driver exactly where we live."

"Gosh!"

"Well, she's got her hands in my flies in no time, and I daren't make a commotion because of the driver, even if it is a big car."

"Yes, the office car."

"You can imagine the rest. We lads don't have much staying power having to be so abstemious, do we?"

"Lord, old chap," Gilbert sympathised. "What did she do then?"

"Well, she got me to do the same for her, and after it I felt revolted, I tell you. I'm scared out of my wits. I think I'm going to have to move to another chummery. Somewhere as far away as possible!"

"That's bad," said Gilbert, "but I can understand it. "I'll back you up, if necessary, with Monty, and we can get someone else I'm sure. Monty's already in bed incidentally."

"Thanks. Oh dear!" Nigel sighed.

The cold weather was very nearly over. The bouts of 'Bombay tummy' which, by one name or another, afflicted newcomers to the land of India, were bothering Gilbert less and less. New situations linked to both business and leisure were becoming routine. He began to feel a part of things, and instead of listening constantly to advice and following precedent he found himself writing home knowledgeably about what was going on around him.

Cotton language at the Trading Ring concerning the receipts of various growths into Bombay, from Central India, Berar, Dhollera, Rajputana and Broach, fired Morton with the desire to travel into the Mofussil, the hinterland, and see for himself the start of it all.

Essentially his meetings with Nigel Bardolf now took place away from Pali Hill. Over a drink at the Gymkhana they discussed local happenings.

"All quiet on the Amorous Tapeworm front, thank

goodness." Nigel said. "Any repercussions your end?"

"Well, actually, she rang up one evening and asked for you. I told her you had left the chummery, but I wasn't sure where you had landed up. She didn't pursue the matter, but made it sound conversational."

"I saw her once down below, milling around the foyer in the interval of a 'flick' at the Excelsior," said Nigel, "so I stayed where I was on the balcony, and went without a drink."

"She sometimes causes embarrassment at the office," Gilbert said. "Came in yesterday, Forbes being in Ahmedabad, and said she wanted the office car and driver to go shopping with a friend, of all things! Poor Meldrum, our number two you know, didn't know which way to turn, but he stuck to his guns and I hope Forbes sees it the right way."

"God, some of these burra memsahibs are the limit," Nigel said. "Doesn't look as if Anita Temple will ever change. By the way, I hear you had to endure an Indian film yesterday. What was it like?"

"Yes, yesterday, I'll tell you about it," said Gilbert. "It was as bad as we hear, and worse.

"I had to go as the guest of Bharat Movietone, associated with the Nandi Mills. Forbes Temple should have gone, of course, had he not been up-country, and others found excuses. It was a Jubilee presentation, and their Excellencies, the Governor and his lady were the only other Europeans there apart from ADCs, their first public attendance at an Indian film.

"I didn't have to meet their Excellencies, but just slid in with my ticket. All the cream of Parsee society was there, an incredible collection.

"Hell, it turned out to be one of the worst ordeals I

have ever been called upon to face. The film was positively ghastly, and went on for hours; it was a sort of allegorical show, all evil spirits, skulls and so on; hardly a thing to take the children to, and interspersed was this shocking Indian music, a horror which words cannot express."

Nigel began to shake with laughter. "I've heard about them," he spluttered.

Gilbert went on: "There was an awful old soothsayer in it, with lungs of brass, who kept up the caterwauling until I longed for a whole box of plasticine to plug my ears.

"Their Excellencies departed during the interval, having been covered in those awful garlands of sickly sweet-smelling flowers which are always produced and flung round people's necks on ceremonial occasions, and when arriving in and leaving the country, and so forth."

"I've seen that," said Nigel. "People seem to take them off pretty smartly."

"Yes, well, I was able to leave after the show was about three quarters of the way through, having then been running a full two and a half hours."

As April, and the hot weather arrived, Bombay started to undergo a distinct change. Princely Rulers began to return to their States up-country. Garden parties and Receptions were over, as were horse shows, polo matches, and other such events. Race meetings were beginning to peter out.

Desirable young females were on their way back home leaving behind the resolute few who were on the brink of marriage. Jaded members of the commercial community, off on home furlough at last, took leave of their envious friends clustered by the gangway of each week's mailboat.

Gilbert got among these well-wishers when he could if only to sample the rare delicacies on board such as Bass beer and a tin or two of Four Square pipe tobacco.

As competition from the young and fair dwindled, the Amorous Tapeworm was heard to be causing concern again among husbands who, though proof by now against her advances, feared the embarrassment and misunderstandings they could produce.

Forbes Temple decided to get his wife off as early as possible this year to the hill station of Mahableshwar favoured by many in Bombay. Up in the Western Ghats not far from Poona which was the retreat of the Governor and his entourage, Mahableshwar was not too far for husbands to spend the odd long weekend there, and the fair sprinkling of Army officers would keep the Amorous Tapeworm occupied in intention if not in deed.

The Temples had an end of season party before Anita departed. All the office men and wives were there besides Gilbert; also the Bowens, and two more youngish married couples he had met once or twice, but no Nigel. Looks like he's made a successful job of staying out of favour, Gilbert thought to himself.

The general theme of conversation was about going 'Home,' or being left behind. Two of the ladies were also going to Mahableshwar; another who was talking about riding, was going to Ootacamund.

"I adore the downland countryside there," she was saying. "Still a bit of malaria about though. Poor Dick and Rachel Young losing their little girl there, or rather at Kodaikanal, last year."

"Yes, so sad," another female voice put in, "but I hear that Rachel is having another try; good for her!"

Some speculation was evidently going on among the Mahableshwar contingent about what they might find there in the way of partners at the Club dances, or company on the small Golf course. When out of Anita's hearing, the two new ladies indulged in making the snide remarks that Gilbert had come to expect about her avid pursuit of males.

"Well, I like a good-looking man as much as anyone," said one of them, "but to be a nympho and show a woman up at her worst is disgusting. It debases all of us."

"Depends on the man a lot," said the other one. "Surely most of them who are any good shy away from such un-selfrespecting and transparent advances as the Tapeworm makes, not to mention her starved appearance, poor thing."

Gilbert thought of the male equivalent of Anita; the sex-at-all-costs type who treated every woman as a pushover, supposedly saying: "Yes, I get plenty of rebuffs, but also a fair number of successes."

The South West Monsoon was always a relief when it broke before the middle of June, and it provided new diversions for Gilbert and others like him. Tennis gave way to squash racquets, and cricket to rugby football, which attracted large crowds of humble Indian spectators who held on to their sides with laughter at the undignified spectacle of sahibs scragging each other in the mud.

There were also the regular 'Mud Sports' for horse riders on the bright days between storms; jumping, tent pegging and milder contests. Finally, golf at the Bombay

Presidency Club.

Gilbert joined in all he could. He had more free time. The cotton season was over until November.

His first monsoon was further improved by finding a pretty little girl who had stayed out with her mother and father. Betty was country born and her father owned a retail business, but her pedigree was genuine enough to pass muster; in addition, she had a longstanding, but fairly loose relationship with another young man which Gilbert saw as a certain safeguard.

He borrowed a car from one of the other fellows now in the chummery, who sometimes had to be away on tour, whenever he could. In this way Betty and he went on several picnics to Trombay. There the paddy fields were flooding. They moved around and across the bunds amid a cacophony of croaking from scores of bullfrogs, newly emerged from their hibernation, and a sickly pale beige colour from their long stay underground.

Everywhere they looked the countryside was already transformed into lush greenery, and there was an influx of birds. Kites were taking a toll of the frogs; vultures, vigilant as ever, perched on budding branches, white egrets were numerous, and partridges, temptingly, uttered their harsh, intermittent calls from the top of hedgerows where the wild lantana flamed.

Betty picked some ground orchids and jasmine, careful of snakes of which they saw two, stalking frogs.

"What do you think of the monsoon's effect out here, Gil?" she asked.

"Amazing, you can almost see things growing. A bit uncanny too; it doesn't seem real, another world, throwing off the last one and preparing for the next. So like the idea of a prehistoric landscape that I wouldn't't be surprised to see a dinosaur come lumbering over that rising ground."

"Ooh, Gil, you are right," Betty said, "I never thought of it that way, but these low lying coastal parts are why, I suppose. Not like the country and forests of the Deccan."

Back in Bombay there were other aspects of the deluging rain which sometimes never stopped for three or four days, flooding drains and menacing the cotton godowns in the Port.

The streets were a sea of black umbrellas. Cars broke down. Gilbert and Monty, on the way to their offices, had to get out and push. The sun broke through and steam rose from the road. They were bathed in sweat beneath their waterproofs and drenched in spite of them.

"Just time to dry out the plugs," said Monty. "God, what a country!"

By mid-September the intervals between the storms were long and more frequent. The memsahibs began to return from the hills.

In the office Forbes looked preoccupied, an air of uncertainty prevailed; then he was off to Bori Bunder to pick up Anita at the Railway station.

Next day she put in an appearance on the way to her first shopping expedition. Gilbert and the others who saw her, stared.

What had happened to the Amorous Tapeworm? She was transformed.

Gilbert buttonholed Nigel in the Gymkhana.

"I can't believe it!" he said. "Anita Temple must have put on about a stone and a half in weight; she looked quite different. Her face and neck have filled out, her arms and shoulders are round and smooth, and her whole figure positively undulates."

"She's been up to something," Nigel said. "What do you think?"

"Like everybody else will, I suppose. She's got herself pregnant."

But as time went by it became evident that Anita was no such thing.

Other memsahibs who had been in Mahableshwar were quizzed excitedly over coffee and dinner tables. None of them had noticed that Anita's activities had been any different from normal, nor could they find a plausible reason for the change in her. The best that one or two could say was that she seemed happier and more relaxed than usual after the first week or two. Forbes, on the two or three visits he had made up there, put it down to the escape from the humid heat and pressures of Bombay.

When anyone has had the reputation that Anita had gained for herself, and the appearance to go with her nickname, such things die hard, and people who have traded on them do not willingly forego their prejudices.

The fact remained that the Amorous Tapeworm was no more. Everything about her had undergone a metamorphosis, and what irked those memsahibs who found her for the first or second time a leader in fashion and beauty, was that Anita hardly seemed conscious of what had taken place.

Maddeningly she had regained her poise and lost her licentiousness. Vainly her rivals tried to create or look for a cause, being something in line with her fixed reputation. No liaison was uncovered. No lover looking for her appeared on the scene. No doctor or psychiatrist could be said to have had a hand in it.

Anita, her beauty enhanced by being more mature, had a new charm and the graciousness of restored pride. It stayed with her throughout the next cold weather season and beyond.

The big boss had been out and was pleased with what he found. Forbes Temple, Gilbert's first burra sahib, was promoted back to England, a definite encouragement to all in the office.

The Temples left Bombay before Mahableshwar could reveal any secrets that might lie there.

# THE CONSTANT MEMSAHIB

It was November in one of the declining years of the British Raj. I had some accumulated leave and decided that, after enough weekends combing the jungles of the Western Ghats for anything in size from button quail to sambhar and panther, I had to try for, and at least see, my first ever tiger.

I wrote to the Divisional Forest Officer at Hoshangabad and obtained permission to reserve and shoot in a block of forest at a location not far from the small hill station of Pachmarhi where there was at least one comfortable small hotel, a sizable European community, and even a Golf course of sorts.

I got off the train at a place called Pipariya and caught the country 'bus which ran several times a day along a valley through a teak forest where my block was, and then on, winding upwards, to Pachmarhi.

A few two storey bungalows situated in glades off the road came into view as the 'bus drew nearer to its destination.

They might have been anywhere, so remote did they seem, and I wondered who lived here.

I found out about one of them due to rather an extraordinary experience I'd had the night before. I'd been down talking to Devi Prasad Prabhaker, the Forester assigned to my forest block, about the movements of any tiger in the vicinity, and what best to do about it.

It was after dark when I caught the last 'bus up the hill, so I sat in front near the driver, nursing my rifle, a .355 Mannlicher carbine. Nothing showed up in the headlights apart from a mongoose and a small civet cat, but on rounding a corner a panther was sitting right in the middle of the road about 60 yards ahead. I signalled the driver to stop, and the hum of conversation among the other dozen or so passengers stopped too, as they stared up the road.

I opened the door silently, got out and fired from rather an awkward position over the nearside front mudguard of the 'bus. The panther jumped up and span round like a top, raising a cloud of dust. Then it straightened out and shot off the right hand side of the road into some bushes.

This put me in a spot. With more than a dozen pairs of eyes following me, after changing to my shotgun and loading it with buckshot, I set off up the road and cautiously approached the point where the panther had disappeared, first looking for drops of blood with my torch and then shining it down a steep bank by the roadside. I could find nothing and see little in the obscurity. The bank fell away gradually. No shining eyes looked into the beam of my torch. No spotted body was curled up or hunched against a tree trunk. I reckoned that I had passed my tests of rectitude and courage and returned thankfully to the 'bus to continue the journey.

The next morning I was due to move into my forest quarters for the days of sport I had arranged for myself. En route, I felt I must leave the bus and visit the scene of the previous night's adventure. I got off as near to the place where it had happened as I could guess, and, after walking both down and back up the road from there, I found where the panther had churned up the dust of the road, so I went to look down the bank. No animal was there, dead or alive, but a cold shiver ran down my spine when I saw, rather to the right of where I had shone my torch, and not more than ten feet down the slope, a flattened area of grass beside a fallen tree trunk where some animal had obviously been resting. After a careful look around I approached it and saw what could be a couple of small bloodstains, but that was all. I was convinced then that the panther was not badly hurt and had got clean away.

Not far up the road was one of the isolated bungalows I had seen. I decided to pay it a visit and mention the slight chance that there might be a wounded animal in the vicinity. Off the road and round a bend was a solidly built white wooden fence with open slats of the kind seen enclosing large paddocks in the English countryside. An equally substantial double white gate and a side gate barred my way on to a rather neglected gravel drive which bisected a luxuriant tropical garden with a small pond visible on the left and a clump of mango trees on the right.

I went through the side gate and as I did so a woman, obviously the lady of the house, came into view from beyond the mango trees which effectively screened the entrance to the bungalow.

She was an arresting sight; though looking any age between 55 and 65 she had the agile gait and upright bearing of an athletic younger woman, but her appearance was distinctly compelling. She was tall and dressed all in khaki except for a sleeveless woollen cardigan of lighter colour. Khaki drill skirt, a mannish cotton shirt with the sleeves rolled up, thick leather belt, leather ankle boots and knee-length wool stockings.

I quickened my stride towards her and held out my hand. "Good morning, I am Dan Marshall," I said. She replied, in a clear but pleasantly feminine voice, and showing just the right amount of interest, "Madge

Arnott-Granger, how d'you do."

I had sent the rest of my things on down with the bus, but was still holding my shot-gun. I saw Mrs Granger – I hadn't caught the first half of her name – looking at it.

"You must excuse me for this early call," I said, "but I had a shot at a panther on the road near here on my way up to Pachmarhi in the 'bus last night, and I thought I should take a look around. I don't think I hit it," I lied, "but your house being so near, it seems right to mention it."

Mrs Arnott-Granger didn't seem in the least bit surprised, but bent down and patted a large and amiable dog which had trotted up to us. "There are always panthers roving round here," she said imperturbably, "looking for a dog or a chicken. But you're a bit too big aren't you, Matt?" She stoked the dog's head, adding, "I thought I heard a shot or a backfire."

Here was the acme of an indefatigable memsahib entrenched in her surroundings, and as much a part of India as the jungle setting in which she lived.

It intrigues me to speculate on the background of people who must have lived a story, and as, anxious not to miss the next bus down the hill, I took my leave of Mrs Arnott-Granger, I was deciding, if I had the time after my 'shikar,' to ask around after her at Pachmarhi.

As it happened I struck lucky at the Golf Club, of all places, where, after a few drinks, a retired Major Calthorpe, once a fellow officer of the late Col. Arnott-Granger, told me enough to enable me to piece the story together.

Madge Warren was the product of a good English Girls' Public School, and a Seminary for young ladies on the edge of Lake Geneva in Switzerland. Her parents had a large country house and led the sort of life that went with it, common to people who were designated as 'County.' The daughters of such families either longed to get away from the isolated feeling it gave them, or happily immersed themselves in the world of horses and graceful social events, from the inside of stables to Hunt Balls. Madge belonged to the last category, and graced it well, being tall, strong and lithe of body, and beautiful of face.

Not long before the end of the last century when the ageing Queen Empress still sat firmly on her throne, Madge came down the gangway of the P & O SS *Malabar* on to the Bombay dockside, and immediately entered the microcosmic world of India. The wide white topee with veil that she wore as purveyed by London's best, though often fanciful, tropical outfitters, was luckily entirely correct. Correctness is so important in India.

A tall, well-built young man detached himself from the milling crowd of coolies, stevedores, native servants and officials on the quayside. He was dressed in the khaki uniform and slim white topee of a sub-inspector of police. Madge jumped up and down and waved her free arm.

"Hello Tim, hooray!" she shouted, and was soon at his side and hugging him.

"Madge!" her brother, Timothy Warren, surveyed her. "You look marvellous, one completely forgets what an English complexion and nice, fresh, clothes look like until the Cold Weather mailboats start to arrive with the 'Fishing Fleet.'" He grinned mischievously.

"Don't jump to any conclusions; I can't see myself getting left behind here so easily," Madge assured him, "but there were some nice chaps on the boat, including a few policemen."

"As a matter of fact I am here also to meet a couple of them who are going back to Poona with us," Tim said. "Come and wait inside here while I see if I can spot them."

He led her to a bench in the Customs hall and left. She sat fascinated with what she saw going on around her, but it wasn't only that; it was something about the whole atmosphere that seemed to be stamping itself on her consciousness, quite unlike any impression she ever had before. She had been in seaports, she had been, in the heat of August, in southern Europe, but it wasn't just either of those ingredients. There was something exotic about it which she couldn't define. The places they had stopped at en route had been different enough, but, she reflected, this country was already suggesting something all of its own, and maybe carrying some kind of a message to her. Strange to have this feeling so instantaneously. Perhaps it was the contrast between the self-contained shipboard life and setting foot all at once on such a seething piece of solid ground.

She recognised the people coming through, now encircled by baggage and heading towards the Customs barrier. Some of them looked back at her, acknowledging her with a smile or a gesture, but, she thought, I am already emerging from a temporary, and soon to be unrecollected time capsule. And this is how I am beginning to feel about the voyage out. She also thought, I must learn the language if I want to become a part of all this.

Tim appeared at her side. "I've got the two new chaps fixed up," he said, "and given them their train tickets. Same one that we'll be on. Leaves about four this afternoon, and should get to Poona just before dark."

Madge found Mr and Mrs Harold Fletcher I.C.S., who gave her a nice bedroom in their bungalow in the large Cantonment, very kind, but somewhat serious and hidebound. Back home, even the stiffer occasions seemed informal compared with some of the evenings when more senior Government officials than Mr Fletcher were on the guest list for dinner, often bringing their own servants to swell the numbers of those posted round the table. It was colourful. She was on nearly all the exchange visits, and usually Tim was there too. His duties had slackened off a bit, now that the Governor had returned to Bombay, and the Social and Sporting calendar was starting there in earnest with the Cold Weather.

Christmas was not far ahead and the Police would be running a Camp for the best part of a week at an ideally situated beauty spot called Lake Arthur Hill. "It will be the third year running," Tim said. "There's quite good shooting, and fishing for trout and mahseer."

It is not unusual for something to happen which dictates the course someone's life is going to take. I don't mean an accident, a death or the loss of money or position, but a feeling that a place gives, or a chance meeting, or even a premonition. In the case of Madge Warren it must have been that first Christmas, and it is understandable.

Christmas cards, as many still are, were either of Winter landscapes, people skating, holly and robins, or religious ones depicting men trudging across a hot looking desert towards a star in the East, or similar arid scenes.

Madge, of course, saw Christmas as the way we know it

at home, but wondered what the other, really more authentic kind, would be like.

Preparations for the Camp had reached the raising of the last large marquee when Tim, Madge and the two young policemen who had been on the Boat got out of the open car. The camp site was ideally placed on a promontory jutting out into the lake, among a number of large and shady trees. Across the lake, and to the side was a high, craggy hill known as Kalsubai with a shrine on its peak.

The Camp was bustling with activity. Dignified, strapping native police officers, their khaki turbans adding to their height, were directing vehicles carrying food, stores and furniture, and putting the finishing touches to the tents.

It was in the days and nights that followed that a kind of enchantment must have fallen on Madge. India has the reputation of weaving a spell on some people, but often this is only realised in retrospect. Not many have had the chance to be enthralled in a short, decisive time.

When the sun went down the evening and night temperatures dropped sharply, the atmosphere had a smell of settled dust and wood fires, and the sky was the clearest Madge had ever seen. There was not even a faint breeze, the moon shone over the lake and the stars alone were almost bright enough to read by.

The native police officers frequented their own Mess tent, but other people moved around, bearers and other Camp servants, among them men from a village near at hand. As it grew cooler they put their blankets over the thin puggrees on their heads so that they came down round their knees and only their faces and legs showed. Silhouetted against the camp fires and in and out of the shadows cast by the rising moon, they looked exactly like figures out of the Bible, Madge thought. In fact, she realised she had never felt so close to the Christmas story before, and of course, this was because here was so much more the atmosphere in which it had all taken place.

She walked into the deep shadow of a tree and prayed, asking for nothing, but rather thanking God for her being able to attribute the deep feelings of recognition which had come to her to this almost magical example of the East, which quite unexpectedly had impressed itself on each one of her senses.

It was still there in the morning. Everything by day contributed in equal share to the unmistakable atmosphere which had started to envelop her with the coming of twilight.

She shared her tent and the bathroom tent behind it with a girl who was engaged to a captain in the Poona Horse who couldn't be there because he had Adjutant duties. Besides this nice girl all the rest of the women were wives with husbands in the Police. Madge found that they were already quite stereotyped in their outlook and conversation, but within this she could discern more than a vestige of pride and affection for India.

Seeing all at once so many facets of up-country life, scrambling up Kalsubai, riding, swimming in the lake, hearing about, and looking at what fish the men had caught, and what game they managed to shoot; hare, duck, teal, partridge, and a strange looking antelope called a Nilghai which only the untouchable jungle charcoal burners would help to deal with or eat because its name meant Blue Bull. All this had its effect on her.

Some people who have found themselves in India for one reason or another are content to abide by all the rules of behaviour and custom laid down, often not without good reason, by their predecessors. This applies more particularly to Europeans who stay in the large towns and seaports where the daily round is a succession of happenings linked to business, sport and entertainment, a lot of it naturally emulating what has been left behind in the home country. That is not to say that there are not enquiring minds fascinated by what India reveals to them if they take the trouble to delve even a little bit.

Up-country, with the natural more rural life of India going on around them, expatriates grow either to love it or despair of it; often, uncomprehending, taking to the bottle.

Madge Warren returned to Poona with Tim, her brother. The place was large enough to offer some sophistication, but inevitably most activities were centred on the Army. The Fletchers were friendly with a Major and Mrs Arnott-Granger of the Poona Horse, and through this she got all the riding she could wish for. She found herself following the tracks and hilly paths which led her instinctively back into the atmosphere which had so got to her at Lake Arthur Hill. She began to be guided by a spiritual consciousness which she easily accepted as wholly subjective. There is no need for me to try and explain, she thought, why it is this that is going to hold me to this changeless country. Marriage, as I knew from the start, would never be my sole reason to stay.

Quite surprisingly Mrs Fletcher, a woman of about 40 already torn between her daughter at school in England and being accustomed to the life she herself had adopted turned out to be, if a little surreptitiously, quite able to share in Madge's feelings. When approached by someone else in a completely natural and artless way, not many people are so self-conscious that they cannot respond likewise, some perhaps more slowly than others.

"The trouble with me, Madge," Kitty Fletcher explained, "is that so much of my time is taken up with Harold's affairs and the rather narrow limits governing them that I don't have much chance to live a life of my own, and if I did I would be interested in India for itself and not just about running it. All the same, I don't hope I will get like Stella Arnott-Granger even if she is a sort of friend of mine. The Major, her husband, pushed by her, even if he does drink to excess, will probably be the C.O. one day and she fulfils every requirement of the Colonel's wife!"

Next time the Arnott-Grangers came in, Madge watched them. Sure enough Stella, by staying behind the Major, whose name evidently was Tony, and propelling him forward, still was able to convey the impression that he was the one who mattered, with admirable showmanship.

The Major himself seemed to be content enough merely just to be convivial, and each time he lingered too long in one group happily re-filling his glass, Stella would materialise saying "Tony, you must meet . . .," or, "Here's so and so; he wants to know how you enjoyed visiting the Mess of the Deccan Horse in Secunderabad."

Madge couldn't help wondering about Tony Arnott-Granger. Admittedly, Army officers were young at this time so that to be a Major in the Indian Army between the ages of 35 and 40, or even younger, was not a bit unusual. The man himself was nice looking, a fine horseman, and competent polo player she heard. He did not yet obviously show any of the ravages of drinking at all. She wondered if any of it was malicious gossip, and found herself becoming interested to know if there was anything behind it, and that a key to it lay somewhere.

Among his other pursuits Major Arnott-Granger naturally enjoyed Hunting, and was, in fact, Honorary Secretary of the Poona and Kirkee Hounds, a Hunt mostly supported by Army officers and those of the Poona Horse in particular.

When Madge first arrived, the Hunt was not operating for the reason that nearly all the hounds were shared with the Bombay Hunt, which completely took them over during their cold weather season from December to March, after which the pack was brought up the hill again for the season in Poona.

Tony Arnott-Granger had, of course, noticed Madge's riding abilities, and the subject of hunting did the rest to start a conversation. Not many ladies hunted astride at that time, and the Major jokingly referred to it when he met her at the horse lines after she had been out one morning hacking. Wearing a newly tailored pair of jodhpurs and a healthy flush on her cheeks, Madge was enough to turn anybody's head, and the Major coughed and coloured when he approached her.

"Have you done any hunting in England, Miss Warren?" he ventured, "and do the ladies ride astride there more now, especially the young and beautiful go-ahead ones?" He put on an arch look which Madge ignored.

"Yes," she answered, "my parents live in Gloucestershire and they both hunt with the VWH, the Vale of the White Horse Hunt, so I have been out half a dozen times since I left finishing school in Switzerland. I don't know, but I think about half the ladies use side-saddle, mostly the older ones, but they are going out."

"I wonder how you'd like it here?" the Major mused, "there's a fair amount of stony ground and nasty patches of sheet rock, and most of the jumps are over cactus hedges; it plays hell with y' boots. We hunt jackal, bagged more often than not. It gets too hot to use up much time drawing coverts for natural 'Jack' even if we do start at sun-up."

"You don't start until the end of March, do you?" said Madge, "so I don't expect I'll be here."

Tony Arnott-Granger blended understanding and disappointment in his look. "Must say 'goodbye,' I'm helping some VCOs to exercise the horses just now."

It was well known that the Major was very well liked by the Viceroy's Commissioned Officers of the Regiment, most of whom were Mohammedans. Naturally, he spoke Urdu well, but better than most British officers. Tim had told Madge about this, adding that as these VCOs hardly ever touched alcohol, Major Arnott-Granger's reputed over-addiction seemed rather unlikely.

Despite what Kitty Fletcher had said, Madge was not convinced, and she found herself drawn to the Major for some reason, possibly to prove something one way or the other.

Now some memsahibs, when they have become accustomed to India, take on a mantle of imperious superiority which does not seem to mellow as long as their husbands still have a possibility of rising in the world. Sometimes they assist this possibility, sometimes hinder it. Stella Arnott-Granger was such a person. She carried it too far, and thus her husband gave the impression of being rather stupid and needing pushing. All that it meant, as Madge came to realise, was that Tony did not measure up to Stella's own high ideals, nor, in fact, did he think much of them.

Pressed by Tim and the Fletchers to stay for the social season in Poona, Madge agreed to do so. In fact, no persuasion was needed as the enchanting atmosphere of India increased its hold on her the more she became able to communicate with all classes of Indians, and see into the lives of the most humble. In this she found an ally in Tony Arnott-Granger as well as the cautious Kitty Fletcher. "One has to be so careful not to lose caste," Kitty reminded her.

Madge learned to be discreet, and not to talk freely about her thoughts and impressions, nor say where she went to when out riding through fields and villages.

Stella Arnott-Granger was, among other things, fearless and aggressive on horseback, notably when out with the Hunt, resplendent in full black habit and veil, on the huge side-saddle which looked most insecure to Madge.

To Tony's evident satisfaction Madge had already been out with the Hunt twice, before the day on which the tragedy occurred, but this time a flying stone had lamed her horse some way off and she had no option but to dismount and walk it back to Camp. On arrival there, a sense of foreboding came to her, and after handing the horse over to the syce she joined a knot of members who were talking in hushed voices.

It seemed that Stella Arnott-Granger had been up with the huntsman when some hounds had gone into the river and started swimming across, but the river was full and fast flowing. The huntsman followed the hounds in and despite his protestations and shouts of warning from Tony, the Master and other members of the field who had come up to the bank, Stella went in further down to head the hounds off. This, to everyone's admiration, succeeded, and hounds and huntsman scrambled back out. Stella, in doing the same, got on to a too-steep soft piece of bank, down which her horse slid backwards, and collapsed tipping her off; weighed down by her heavy sodden habit and boots, she disappeared.

By the time Madge walked into the Camp, Stella's body had just been recovered. Her horse, with the heavy side-saddle, drowned too.

Tony obtained leave to convey his wife's body back to England on the next mailboat from Bombay, and as a mark of respect hunting was suspended until after the monsoon.

The tragedy was discussed throughout the Station for a couple of weeks, and then the subject died down, so that by the time Tony Arnott-Granger returned everybody had had their say and were now wondering what he would do with himself. Would he, for instance, released more completely into the Officer's Mess, go rapidly to the dogs of drink? Or had the tendency been caused by his wife's overbearing ways?

The other memsahibs in the Cantonment made the usual sort of kindly effort while penetrating his household from time to time, and coming back with the news that when he was at home Tony's habits seemed unchanged and unremarkable. Madge Warren saw him often enough. At parties and gatherings he was boisterous, intoxicated and rather silly. On his own he was listless even with her. She attempted to coax him out of it.

He turned a longing gaze on her and smiled wanly. "Madge, you're only just experiencing all the things that go with the life of the Army and the Civil Service on stations in India, but I have had enough of it after fifteen years. It doesn't go anywhere near the heart of India. I think the only time I felt that I had a place was when the Battalion was up on the North West Frontier.

There was, of course, danger, but that is what we came here to face sometimes. Otherwise, it was all real and natural. Our own lives and hearts were in the right environment. I drank only at the end of the day when it was earned and needed. Here in Poona I can't get away long enough from boredom. Stella, of course, took to this life utterly as her father and grandfather were both in the Indian Army, but now I would like to be free of the socialising and the drinking which is the only way I seem able to get through the dreary evenings. Poor Stella, of course I miss her, but the artificiality of it all never seemed to strike her."

"Even though I have only been here for a short time," Madge said, "it seems to me that India has a way of putting Britons who spend a good part of their lives here in a sort of dilemma. I have noticed it in at least three or four people, and now you. What I mean is that they seem to be torn between a growing love and curiosity for the country and, despite the contrasts between rich and poor, the magic that it seems to hold in the atmosphere generated by ancient lore and steadfast faith, while on the other hand as Imperial delegates, they have to acknowledge the need to conform to a very rigid tried code of social conduct and exemplary behaviour which does not give them much time except to be conscious of their own roles."

"You are right," said Tony, "it is a magic land, and people are fools to keep up the pretence of needing to look down on the way Indians live and behave, judging them by their own expatriate standards instead of investigating their way of life, and letting themselves be carried along a bit by what is revealed to them. Fortunately, there are men and women in our history who have warded off the taboos and enriched the world through their revelations of India."

Before the end of June, in view of the sad interruption of what should have been a busy and happy season, Madge returned to England.

She wrote to Kitty Fletcher who told her in reply that, to everyone's surprise, Major Arnott-Granger, instead of waiting for the promotion which was only a matter of time for him, they thought, provided he took care of himself, had accepted a transfer to the new 19th Hyderabad Regiment which was being formed in the Nizam's dominions to replace the Hyderabad Contingent, an irregular body of men set up almost a century ago with European officers, mainly British.

Major Calthorpe had only arrived in Poona as a subaltern a few weeks before Madge Warren came, he said, and the Mess gossip was then a bit over his head, but before Arnott-Granger went off to Hyderabad he heard that he had kept in touch with Madge, obtaining her address from Kitty Fletcher.

Madge, as it turned out, had been restless back in Gloucestershire and could not get India out of her mind. Secretly, she must have decided that Tony Arnott-Granger would be her passport back. Indeed, the two letters she had had from him were enticing in themselves, and he seemed like a new man.

Back with the Fletchers, she did not stay long, Major Calthorpe told me, and was soon on her way to Hyderabad. She and Tony were married two months later, and for ten years until he was retired not much more was heard about them in Poona.

It was known that they had been back home on leave a couple of times. Also that, according to Kitty Fletcher, Madge had had a miscarriage on one of these home visits.

Then Calthorpe said he was moved from Poona to Meerut where he joined the Tent Club and got thoroughly involved in Pig-sticking, which caused the limp I noticed he had.

All the same, the news seeped through that Arnott-Granger, upset at the loss of his child, had resumed his heavy drinking, had put on a lot of weight, and was far from fit.

All had gone well at first; Tony adored Madge, as well he might, and the enchantment she had found in the jungle trails round Lake Arthur Hill that first Christmas, and even over the Poona Hunt country, she soon knew was only the beginning of it.

To the north of Hyderabad State where it becomes Berar, the Tapti River flows and the countryside as far as eye could see is dominated by the Satpura Hills, wild and beautiful.

Just as had happened in Poona, the Indian officers and other ranks took to Lt. Col. Arnott-Granger, as he had now become, and because in so many ways the Regiment was answerable to the Nizam, its British officers were less bound by convention to segregate themselves. Madge found that this freed her from being restricted to the usual narrow social circle and its risks to Tony, and enabled her to involve herself in the welfare and lives of all ranks.

It was just what she wanted. As the Colonel's wife, not only could she draw some of her own guidelines, but she did not have to concern herself so much with what the more junior officers and their wives, some of whom were older than she, did with themselves, or thought.

Tony frequently had to leave Hyderabad city and operate from one or other of the large semi-permanent camps the new Regiment would use round the State boundaries, mostly to the north.

Early on she tackled her husband as he left for a tour of duty.

"Tony," she said, "I didn't come here to be separated from you, why can't I go with you? You know how we both feel about the real life and pulse of India and here we are on the threshold of it all."

"Well, darling, it is still part of the Indian Army that I am in, you know. They make the rules, but let me think about it when I am up in Hingoli," was the Colonel's reply. "Mustn't set any wrong precedents. Nor is it decided how we will operate now in that area."

"What is at Hingoli?" Madge asked.

"It is the Cantonment occupied as headquarters by the Hyderabad Contingent for the whole of its existence, but now it is to be abandoned, being unnecessarily cut off in these days of better mobility."

Eventually it was decided not to dismantle the Hingoli Cantonment entirely, but leave a small garrison there and keep it as an outpost and supply depôt.

Even in 1859 when large bodies of rebels from the Mutiny were still menacing the region and had to be disarmed or destroyed, Hingoli was not attacked. Still less were dacoits, pindaris or criminal tribes likely to come out of their haunts and hideouts while Hingoli was manned.

Accordingly Madge had her way, having become even more insistent, in the meantime, as well as extracting more about the historical background of the territory on the northern borders of Berar from officers in the Deccan Horse whose Cantonment at Secunderabad almost adjoined that of the Hyderabad Regiment in Golconda, and whose Mess provided a well established social centre.

In the course of this, she met a very old retired Jemadar of the Hyderabad Contingent who could remember stories going back as far as when it was founded in 1813.

Conversing in a mixture of Urdu and English, Jemadar Murjat Ali told Madge tales of the Mahratta and Pindari wars and of the emergence and prowess of Arthur Wellesley, first as a Lieut. Colonel in command of the Hyderabad forces, and then a General marching into Aurangabad and defeating the Mahratta hordes at Assaye.

These early years were quite vital to Madge she had told Major Calthorpe since coming to Pachmarhi, so much so that she knew she could never keep away from India whatever its future.

Even to me, whom she would call a city dweller, the feeling I got when ensconced in my Forrest block, named East Jhiria, was one of being enclasped within it all, and at the same time lord of it, my subjects Arcadian villagers pathetically content in their simplicity, and unstirred by social unhappiness and the demands of democracy.

I could imagine Madge's reactions on learning that a viceroy of the Mogul Emperor Aurangzeb made his capital at Deogiri and changed its name by command to Aurangabad. Riding with Tony on paths skirting some of the most impenetrable jungles and forested hills in the whole of India. Gazing at the cavernous rock temples of Ellora and the huge statues hewn out among them. Then Ajanta; Jemadar Murjat Ali said that in the time of his grandfather, and even after his father too had joined the Contingent, although Mahratta armies and other invaders poured through the passes of the Ajanta Hills, the wonderful rock-hewn sanctuary of Buddhist monks with its caves and halls, and fabulous painted murals, had not yet been revealed. Riding up to them on a path which too must have been then entirely overgrown, Madge felt an exciting, if humble, reverence.

Tony Arnott-Granger was never fitter nor more absorbed, both in his wife and his duties, than at this time. A further company of Cavalry was added to the Regiment and, because of his all round experience, Tony was accorded the rank of brevet Colonel.

It helped to reassure Madge that she could not have chosen a better path to discovering what she had instinctively known India would hold for her. The two years that had gone by had strengthened the realisation that the growing bond was already binding her in a very personal, almost exclusive way.

She knew that she was very different from the classic Colonel's wife that Stella would have been. True, she was sensible enough not to treat the servants any differently than they, or custom, expected, but she had no preoccupation with home leave and home fads and fashions as did the other wives; nor did she try over much to reproduce 'Home' inside the bungalow.

Tony did not seem to regard these things as shortcomings, and a number of junior officers, their lives restricted, from necessity or otherwise, to the pursuit of physical ends, found Madge's company and conversation much to their liking.

For his part, Tony had been too busily engaged up-country in re-organising the defence of the Nizam's northern boundaries. The country there, as Madge had seen for herself, was ideal cover for marauders and was seldom quiet from their raids and attacks on villages. Preventive forays were part of the Regiment's main action against these bands, either of Brinjaras, normally peaceful, but untrustworthy, or Pindaris, a warlike community of freebooters, constantly a source of trouble, besides other outlaws able, one way or another, to bear arms and seeking to annex land, as also the Thugs and dacoits who menaced peaceful jungle aborigines and law-abiding villagers.

Colonel Arnott-Granger was in his element organising these assignments to subjugate and pacify all such enemies of the Nizam, but that done, his position and responsibilities, including being an ADC to HEH, meant that he must put a time limit on his absences from headquarters in the Cantonment.

This worried Madge, for she knew that it was her fascination for the Country which had prompted her to stay, and not infatuation with Tony. Seeing him as he was in Poona had awakened in her a female desire to help him to mend his ways and strengthen his character. As in Poona he had been able to foster the same regard that his men felt for him as a soldier and a considerate and resolute leader, but as a man he was obviously weak, and this is what Madge knew she resented.

She thought that probably Stella had, after all, been better for him. A strong minded woman, but in quite a different way from Madge who tried to treat Tony with loving patience, rather than Stella's almost contemptuous pillorying of him. Or had this made him more inclined to atone for his social shortcomings with drink?

A severe bout of malaria brought Tony back to the Cantonment at Golconda ahead of time. Madge, who had been on her own for more than a month, welcomed the diversion, and, finding herself truly in the role of a Burra-memsahib, acquitted herself well, not only with the well-wishers of the Regiment, but also frequent callers from Secunderabad. As the quinine did its work, Tony had plenty of chance to substitute pegs of whiskey.

After two years, I am getting more and more irritated by Tony, Madge thought to herself, I wish he would not be so polite and ingratiating with me.

It was all right while they were adventuring together on horseback, and she felt kindly enough, almost sentimental, when he was away on his own, but within two days of his return the irritation came back again. She felt bad about it and that made matters worse. Shades of Stella!

Madge, true to her breed, was not a very sexually conscious person, and Tony, not improved by drink, had not been able to arouse in her what could be there in the right hands. Madge knew that she had never been in love, but had not made it one of her priorities to wait for the unlikely fairy prince. She was in the environment she sought whether he was likely to be found in it or not.

The trouble with Tony was that he could see Madge

slipping away from him, but seemed to have no idea what he himself could do to stop it. To Madge, it was as if he thought that his wife, some fifteen years younger, still had time enough to develop a mind of her own. In fact, he was the indecisive one.

"Tony," Madge said, not for the first time, "why don't you treat me more as a friend and partner, and take me into your confidence that way? I am not just a sort of ornament to be where I look best."

"Oh, but you are, dear," said Tony," and I don't have anything to confide that you don't know about."

"Then, what do you say if I tell you that I am 2 months pregnant?"

"Well, bless my soul! That is good news. We must make arrangements." He came over and kissed her. "Let's have a drink on that."

"All right, not just yet for me anyhow," said Madge, "but what arrangements?"

"For you to go home and have the baby."

"But why not, say, to Bombay?"

"Because dear, no European army wife of any consequence at all can have her children born in India, or even on the boat within the three mile limit. If that happened it would mean the child is Country born."

"How on earth would that matter, Tony?" Madge expostulated.

"Because it would be like the ordinary British soldier who risks his children being seen as Eurasians which, of course, they often are."

"You sound as if you would insist on getting me away?" Madge asked.

"Well, it's not me; I am trying to explain to you how these things are." Tony looked troubled, and Madge, ironically, found herself preferring him to be cross and uncompromising.

"I think I will be able to come with you." He finished by saying: "It wasn't exactly a proper furlough I had last time I was home."

Madge was unhappy about having to travel in the heat down to Bombay and then the long voyage, but more so about her India not being where her baby was born. She had, and lost, the baby two months later in England. It was a boy. Tony left her there and returned to see out the Hot Weather.

Madge did not know if she really wanted a family before, realising how much it would change her chosen way of life into what she could see others around her leading in the Cantonments. Now, after one experience, she had no wish to try again, knowing as she did that she did not love Tony enough for it.

Mess life, and the Hot Weather, were not good for Col. Arnott-Granger, and, as Major Calthorpe had said, that, and the loss of the child started him off on drinking again, and it was not something he could easily disguise.

If not actually seeing any more than did anyone of the reclusive Nizam, he was, by virtue of his duties as an ADC to the austere Mohammedan Ruler, not a little involved with the mounted cavalry who formed the bodyguard of His Exalted Highness, most of whom were Moslems, besides an infantry force composed of Arab descendants of one time Mahratta mercenaries. For members of the Court alcohol was banned. Outside their Messes, it behoved British officers to be discreet.

Col. Arnott-Granger need not ordinarily have retired at fifty but, plagued by an enlarged liver, he no longer sat comfortably in his saddle, and left Madge to ride where she willed as she had at the beginning in Poona. She made new friendships in the cool downs of the Nilgiri Hills where she joined the Ootacamund Hunt and had exhilarating gallops over their country where 'Sholas,' wooded hollows, harboured panthers, and occasionally tigers, which were sometimes put up by the hounds. Instead of lasting out the Hot Weather as she had often done Madge found fresh trails in the Nilgiris and made the most of this new face of India.

Meanwhile, Tony's inability to reduce his drinking brought on recurrent attacks of jaundice and this gave his superiors the opportunity to agree with the Nizam's recommendation to have him transferred, and he was invalided out of the Indian Army before worse occurred.

Unlike Stella, who had become increasingly sour and intolerant of Tony's weaknesses, Madge had established her own life and refused point blank to go back to live in Cheltenham or Bath in the vain hope of his recovering his health.

It was she who chose the two storey bungalow, nestling on a spur of hill and overlooking, on its far side, the valleys leading all the way down to Pipariya.

While in Ootacamund Madge made friends with the wife of a man in the Indian Forest Service who had been on the Central Provinces Eastern Circle for a time, and it was they who told her about Pachmarhi.

She knew there was much more social life in the Nilgiris, but also more temptation for Tony and more of a drain on their finances. For herself, one visit to Pachmarhi's forest setting was enough to make up her mind. The Kaiser's war in Europe put that out of reach for Tony anyhow.

She set about making both the bungalow and its

grounds to her liking, and got Tony to see a leading Indian Medical Service doctor in Nagpur. This man gave him a year at most to live, unless he stopped drinking altogether.

During her days in Ootacamund Madge had had her admirers, mostly short-stay single Army officers recuperating from accidents or illness. To her, they had provided escorts until she met Thomas Maudsley, an interesting man and a childless widower, formerly ICS, who managed the Maharajah of Mysore's Arranmore lodge, including the arranging of functions in the magnificent ballroom.

Here was a man who had both feet on the ground, about her own age, nearing his forties, and providing Madge with something new in the shape of a person who was completely normal and uncomplicated, but far from dull, and able to turn his hand to most things.

What is it that makes a person independent, Madge had thought, granted that some people are more content to be on their own than others. If you want it done properly do it yourself. Nevertheless, to find someone self-contented and able, at the same time, to be a good companion was something she had never achieved with the opposite sex, though she had seen enough examples to know that such was not just a fantasy. Tom Maudsley fitted this mould.

Also, while avoiding all the usual banal approaches, one of the things he was able, and more than willing to share, was Madge's bed, which he did on several occasions in a manner entirely satisfactory to them both. The surroundings of Arranmore where this happened were just right for adding the atmosphere of romance essential for Madge to lose herself in, keeping only the shred of common sense that she knew was necessary for her peace of mind about the present and her prospects for the future.

She had been right about this. Many officers and men, both from the Indian Army and States forces were leaving for Europe, and some for East Africa. Tom Maudsley felt the call, and set off for Mombasa on some kind of secondment through Muscat involving the Sultan of Zanzibar.

On moving to Pachmarhi Madge redoubled her efforts to get Tony to take more interest in mapping out this new phase in their lives besides doing something that would improve his health, but it was a losing uphill struggle.

They had brought their khansama, cook, and the syce in charge of two horses, and with some difficulty trained one of these to take harness with a light carriage. After a while the syce learnt to take the reins so that Tony could get back safely from his visits to the Club over the three miles to Pachmarhi.

Tony became morose over the War. "I ought to be there," he said. "Why didn't I play my cards better? I could have gone and been of some good use."

"Tony, you know you couldn't, everything is against you."

"Well, what about old Pat Ryder?"

"Pat passed Staff College in Quetta, and training soldiers is his speciality, you know that, Tony."

"I'm going to try for a Staff job in New Delhi then."

Madge shrugged her shoulders, avoiding further dangerous discussion.

She thought of Tom and wondered if it was because of him she felt this deadness towards Tony now, but decided it had set in well before that when he stopped being his active likeable self after malaria. It was an awful feeling, but unshakeable. She had no desire to touch him or have any physical contact just as one would about a perfect stranger.

She remembered her earlier reactions to Tony's return from his absences from Hyderabad. It was already starting then. He would never be absent now, until . . ., and then she knew she would feel guilty and unhappy with herself – for a time.

It was before he, himself, came here, Major Calthorpe had said, but he heard that Col. Arnott-Granger became more bloated and, deceiving himself that he was over-eating, lost his appetite for food, but not for drink. He died of cirrhosis of the liver about eighteen months after their arrival.

Tom Maudsley had gone into the East African campaign in Tanganyika. Madge received several letters from South Africa including one of condolence, and then they stopped.

Most people who came to Pachmarhi, did so for short periods, avoiding the heat in the plains, and quite a few were from Bombay. Permanent European residents like Madge numbered perhaps no more than fifty, but she had her friends among both categories.

She had no name for aloofness, Major Calthorpe said, and people liked her to be with them, including himself. In fact, she stood out at gatherings, but was natural and unaware of the impact she made.

I could understand it. No memsahib of the substance of Madge Arnott-Granger who had interwoven herself contentedly into the fabric of India will ever stop being a part of it, even if it is their ghosts before whom recalcitrant servants quail. Round the camp fires, as those at Lake Arthur Hill that Christmas, stories will surely be told of them.

As I rattled down the hill for the last time from Pachmarhi I cast a look over my shoulder to where the bungalow was. Nothing moved but a breeze stirring the mango trees. Not even the dog, Matt, was in evidence.

I had not felt like calling again, I don't know why.

# THE GREEN PIGEON

It is a lovely bird, the green pigeon. Perhaps it could be called the wood pigeon of India. It is about the same size. Emerald green on its back, neck and head, the larger wing feathers are of a darker shade, while underneath they range from lemon green to yellow.

It is seen in small flocks, perhaps because its favourite food is the berries which grow in profusion at the top of tall banyan trees and others, where it vies with the flying fox fruit bats for its fair share.

Richard Marsh knew of its value too as a table bird when with friends he had often gone on weekend shoots in the jungles just off Bombay Island in the lower foothills of the Western Ghats. It has lighter flesh than the wood pigeon, and part of the breast at the side is as white as chicken.

But this is not a tale of the jungle and shikar, it has really to do with Kashmir.

Marsh would never have got there had it not been for the War with Hitler's Germany, because normally local leave between long leaves home to Britain meant little more than long weekends, extended at times by Christian, Hindu or Moslem religious holidays, for people who were in Commerce in Bombay, Calcutta, Madras or Karachi. After six war-time years with staffs depleted by conscription to the Indian Army or Navy, those who remained needed a break. The menace of Japan had receded by then, and some people were being demobbed and returning to their wives and civilian occupations.

So Richard got his chance and took off by the Great Indian Peninsula Railway with his bedding roll, but without his Bearer, as far as Murree.

He had some Army friends who were recuperating on a hired houseboat at Srinagar, and the chance was too good to miss. It was May, with the Hot Weather at its height in Bombay, and the monsoon not due for another six weeks.

The winding and bumping journey for most of the day on the rattling 'bus from Murree to Srinagar could obviously have been tedious, but was relieved completely for Marsh by the spectacular scenery that was revealed round every corner of the road as it followed the course of the Jhelum river. Not only that, but the exhilarating freshness of the air wafting down from snow-capped mountain slopes, Marsh thought, literally came from heaven after all the years of sticky heat.

Apart from polite greetings and an occasional comment to the other dozen or so passengers, none of whom were Europeans, but probably families returning home or exchanging a visit to Kashmir, Marsh remained silent, drinking it all in between napping or picking up the book which was the best he had been able to find in the way of a guide.

There were three chaps from the Indian Army sharing the houseboat when Marsh arrived, a Major and two Captains, one of whom had been working in a Bank in Bombay. He was a 'Rajput,' Rajputana Rifles, and the others, Regulars, were respectively a 'Jat' and a 'Gurkha,' following the popular nomenclature for officers whatever the colour of their skins. Marsh's other friend had rejoined his Regiment.

His remaining friend, Bob Wallace, was mainly concerned about his status in the Bank when his turn came, as it looked like doing soon, to return to civilian life.

"What does it look like to you, Dick?" he asked during their first evening meal deftly provided by the khansama.

"Much better than had I been called up, say, last year, to become a subaltern when you were captains and majors and so on," Marsh replied ruefully, "but No, from what I have seen, people like me who have stayed behind have simply done the jobs of two, and fellows coming back have resumed just what their jobs entailed when they left, and in the cases I know of any commensurate salary increases have gone on automatically. You've been drawing your salary, haven't you? Or rather the difference, if any, between it and your Army pay?"

"Yes, that's right," Bob Wallace agreed. "Well, I'm sure I'll be all right. I also think it would be nice to consider getting married after all this business."

The houseboat was moored, with about a dozen others, on the Jhelum within a short walk of the central bazaars of Srinagar. About two thirds of the houseboats were occupied it seemed, maybe more, as Indian families seemed to come and go. Several contained retired middle aged European couples who occasionally had younger visitors, probably members of their family. One such couple, a Mr and Mrs Stringer, next door but one to the 'Rolls Rice', comprised a retired schoolmaster from one of the Lawrence schools, and his wife, also a teacher, who still taught English and History in Srinagar.

Bob said that they were likeable intelligent people, very good to talk to on most subjects, not least about India itself and where it might be going. He was a CIE and she held the Kaiser-i-Hind medal.

The days were full of interest, life and colour, but after dark there was really little or nothing to do. They all sat on the top deck under the canopy, with a couple of Flit guns to hand to ward off the mosquitos, and played cards over a local beer or a bottle of Nasik whisky. Sometimes after dinner they had coffee with the Stringers and chatted.

Richard found that there was more of an atmosphere of awareness of coming changes here in Northern India than in Bombay so much devoted to Commerce with the West and the present War effort. Of course, there were at just this time of the year, the usual communal riots between Hindus and Moslems ebbing and flowing in Bombay's back streets, but here in Kashmir was a majority Moslem population ruled over by a Hindu Maharajah, a cause of overt rumblings from 'Congresswallahs' headed by Abdul Gaffar Khan, the 'Frontier Gandhi.'

"Yes, I can really see Kashmir running into trouble," Mr Stringer was saying one evening. "Gaffar Khan is not at all popular with the Moslems of Jammu who see him as a traitor to their religion. Border skirmishes will develop into full scale fighting if Jinnah keeps sounding off from Karachi about Zindabad."

"It would be ironic if, when nearing the point of getting independence, India was partitioned off into Hindu and Moslem States, wouldn't it?" said Bob Wallace. "We hear the men talking about it sometimes and, of course, as in some other Indian Army Regiments, we have Hindus, Sikhs and Moslems in the Rajputs."

"Places as near as Gulmarg would be close to a

frontier," said Mr Stringer, "I would hate to see any part of Kashmir, so romantic and lovely, turned into a modern battleground."

Richard was interested in Gulmarg. "I want to get at least two weeks up there," he said, "and I'm longing to play golf over both the courses. I have heard they are good and have the most beautiful surroundings in the world."

The Jat and Gurkha officers nodded in assent. They had both played there two years ago.

"But it's too early yet," remarked Mr Stringer, "there will still be a lot of snow on the ground for about a couple of weeks. I've got friends up there already and will let you know."

It turned out as Mr Stringer had said, and Richard decided to hire a bicycle as the best way to get around all that Srinagar and its nearby wonders had to offer, including the gardens of Shalimar, Nishat and Nasim with their flowers, Chenar trees and lakeside peace. To be able to stop where he liked and free to be a part of it all, exploring, seeing and hearing the cascades of melting snow toppling down the blue mountain sides, and returning, pleasantly tired, in the evening was like being in another world.

With a bare two weeks remaining, he left his friends and took a car up as far as the road to Gulmarg safely went, and from there on the only route was up a path through pine woods, either on foot or by donkey. In effect Richard did a bit of both. A porter using a strap in the Tibetan way with a broader part across his forehead, after threading it through the handles of Marsh's case and bedding roll, toted the baggage up the hill in knapsack fashion. Little children, sitting in a basket, were able to accomplish the ascent in the same easy manner Richard saw as he caught up with a small family slightly ahead of him. Pockets of snow still survived in most of the hollows. Others were gathering into small streamlets.

It took over an hour to reach Gulmarg's outskirts up to the point where the porters and donkeymen were paid off for no more than a few rupees.

Two cars were waiting. The family got into one, and the other Richard shared with a seconded I.C.S. man who had beginning of the season things to do preparing the way for the Resident. He said there would already be a bit of life starting up. The Club and Nedou's Hotel were open, and he himself was after a game of golf because there was a competition next week on the lower course. His name was Hamilton. "It is always a bit soon for the greens to be at their smoothest," he said, "but the fairways are ideal after the snows, and the air so good you feel you could hit the ball a mile."

"It sounds great," Marsh agreed, and as they finished by arranging to meet at the weekend, he decided to try out a couple of practice rounds on his own.

Gulmarg, at 8500 feet, is not a bustling hill station, but more of a handy refuge for inhabitants of Srinagar and further afield in the hottest months of the year, besides, at this time, a sprinkling of army officers and wartime officials.

The Maharajah, Sir Hari Singh, has no Summer palace there, and, balked of being able to go to Europe, would go again to Simla, according to Hamilton.

Thus, Richard Marsh hardly realised he had been in the village until he was through it. One unpaved street with a dozen or so of native bazaar shops seemed to be all there was of it. Behind and above the street were a few 'pucca' built masonry buildings, but everywhere else, whether they might be dwellings or commercial premises, the construction was of wooden board walls and asbestos or oilcloth and birchbark roofs weighted down with small boulders or adobe out of which flowers were starting to appear. All had makeshift looking chimneys which evidently served their purpose. A few goats and cattle wandered around, and the smell of smoke from dung fires was not disagreeable.

Hamilton got off in the village, and after about another mile Marsh arrived at the Golf Clubhouse which served as a combined social centre, hotel, pub, restaurant and information office. The visitor's application form and fee were informal and nominal.

Richard soon found himself in a small detached cabin-like wooden chalêt on the hillside. It was cold, water running from melted snow was visible through the raised floorboards of the verandah, small living room and bedroom. There was, however, a wood fire ready laid, besides a number of numdah like floor rugs and plenty of blankets. Strange how blankets became a symbol of something almost magically luxurious in the eyes of anyone confined to the plains and coasts of India. Richard Marsh remembered vividly during one July in Calcutta getting away to Darjeeling for a long weekend and using four blankets. "Four blankets, my dear!" was something to recount back down at the Tollygunge Club.

Marsh was pleased to see quite a crowd of people dining in the Gulmarg Club, made up of both sexes and civilians as well as the Services, though younger officers predominated, eyeing any female up to the age of 55 with faintly disguised hunger: it had been a long time, by

1945. Few women were likely to be unaccompanied, but most were enthusiastically joining in the dancing, and Marsh was willing to bet that a few liaisons, out of many attempted, came off all right.

He noticed a very striking woman, perhaps in her late thirties, sitting at a table with three rather senior looking men. She had beautiful smooth limbs and shoulders and a strong aristocratic face which, though tanned, was not in any way marred by the dry crinkled effect that more mature memsahibs often suffered from in the East when they spent a lot of their time in the open air. She declined a couple of invitations to dance, and did not move from her seat while Marsh was there, so he shot what he considered were discreet glances in her direction for as long as he dare.

On his second evening, he found himself at the Bar talking to the steward, a Col. Dixon who was the same man who had given him his membership form. Evidently he was Secretary/Manager of the Club, and in fact, helped by a younger European and an Anglo-Indian girl in the office, he had a hand in everything it seemed, including the golf.

"Have you tried the course yet, Mr Marsh?" the Col. asked. To which Richard said he had had a few holes. "Quite tough," Richard observed. "Some of the holes are pretty tight, between the pines and the deodars. The surroundings are so beautiful, that perhaps the head comes up too easily!"

Col. Dixon laughed. "By the way," he said, "it is a custom here for every new member to invent a cocktail, and, if it is good enough, we adopt it and put it on the books. No more than one or two a season make it. Like to try?"

Now Richard had a name for his concoctions in the chummery in Bombay, so he reckoned he would.

"Let me know tomorrow," said the Colonel, moving to attend to others who had come up.

During his first round of golf with Hamilton the next day in the late afternoon, not doing too badly with his hired clubs, Richard had time to look around between his long shots, and was fascinated by the number of bright coloured birds he saw. Several different sizes of green parakeets flew noisily over in flocks of up to a dozen, their colour outlined against the breathtaking expanse of snow capped mountains that surrounded the fairway valleys above the dark trees, like a continuous dazzling white frieze which was beginning to be tinged by the going down of the sun.

There were many green pigeons, and a pair of other similar birds decked in brilliant colours from maroon through purple to bottle green, which Hamilton said were Imperial Pigeons, flashed across.

Some of the greens they were reaching towards the end of their round were saucer-shaped platforms to the edge of which the forest crept down. Richard could see what looked like large game birds, brilliantly coloured, appearing on the back apron of the green. Their one 'Agiwallah' (forecaddie) promptly dashed up and shooed the birds away as if they were crows or kites and liable to pick up the balls as happened in Bombay.

"What were those?" he asked Hamilton.

"They would be kaleej pheasants or similar species," Hamilton said. "They come out before dusk for what they can find, and do a bit of damage scratching around, but the agiwallah is just showing off."

"Well, let's keep him with us next time," Marsh

suggested. "I'd like to get a closer look at them, if they are not too shy in their wild state."

As he went round the golf course Richard had been thinking about his cocktail. It would have dry vermouth, something else, say vodka, and just enough crème de menthe to make it a pretty shade of green. Oh yes, and a dash of lemon juice to keep down the sweet minty taste. Then he would call it 'Green Pigeon.'

He detailed the recipe that evening to Col. Dixon. Two parts of the vermouth, one of vodka, two or three dashes of crème de menthe, and a squeeze of lime - better than lemon. They tried it, and the colonel looked impressed. "Right," he said, "this is on the house, and I'll put it as a suggestion on tomorrow's dinner menu card."

Next evening at dinner Marsh ordered a Green Pigeon. He looked around from time to time to see if any more were visible. Only one young woman seemed to have one. He felt a bit disappointed and decided he couldn't keep still watching like this. He lit one of his favourite Burma cheroots and strolled down to the bazaar which had taken on quite a festive look with many oil lanterns and acetylene lamps, but nearly all behind doors closed against the cold night wind. He pulled up his coat collar and turned back to his cabin.

The first thing Col. Dixon said to him, smiling, next day before lunch, and after a mediocre nine holes of golf, caught him unawares.

"Your Green Pigeon was quite a success last night, Mr Marsh."

"Really?" said Richard, brightening, "I didn't wait to see, actually."

"Yes, at least a dozen were ordered. What's more Mrs

Lansdowne liked it and had two."

"Mrs Lansdowne?"

"Our local 'Nanda Devi' and leader in fashion and good taste. She is forthright in her opinions and preferences, but sound, very sound. Looks like the Green Pigeon will stay to roost here! You must have seen Mrs Lansdowne? She was here again last night."

"Oh, the strikingly handsome woman in a red dress who I saw sitting with several men on my first evening here? I must have left before she came last night."

"That was her; I'll introduce you sometime. She's worth meeting." The Colonel drifted off.

It was Hamilton's last night, and Richard decided to ask him about Mrs Lansdowne if he got the chance. He felt he ought to be a little more prepared for the lady.

He had, in fact, asked Hamilton to join him for dinner, saying he would wait for him at the Club bar, so that if work held him up it didn't matter.

Richard liked sitting at the bar as from there, he could see all the comings and goings between the lounge and the dining room. In this way he had already got a good feel of the place. Col. Dixon was not there when he arrived early. The Sikh regular barman and the young fair man, probably country born, were bustling around. Several people either sitting, or ordering drinks and taking them away, passed the time of day with him.

Then Col. Dixon appeared, and suddenly, behind him, he heard a rather husky but melodious voice ask for a 'Green Pigeon." With a start Richard recognised who it was, and Col. Dixon said: "Right, Mrs Lansdowne, and here, as it happens, is the creator of it, Mr Marsh from Bombay. Mr Marsh, meet Mrs Lansdowne."

"Hello, Mr Marsh," she said. "I do like your drink and

it's clever name. Do you mange to go on shikar and enjoy the wildlife you can still see in the jungles outside Bombay? My late husband was Conservator of Forests for a time at Nasik."

This was a subject in which Marsh felt well at home and he relaxed a bit despite realising that Mrs Lansdowne was swiftly taking him in.

"Yes, I go whenever I can, helped by a Naval friend who can get enough petrol coupons," he replied, and he thought of places like Khardi, Bapsai, and Parali for which he had often had permits from the Divisional Forest Officer of the same Northern Circle to use the Inspection Bungalows, especially coveted for Christmas or Easter.

But his answer was enough for Mrs Lansdowne who said to him: "You must try to explore the valleys around here, Mr Marsh," and collecting her drink she floated off as if modelling her plain kingfisher blue ankle length dress.

Hamilton turned up not long after, and they found a good table at the side of the dining room.

"I don't have any personal experience of Lucille Lansdowne," said Hamilton in answer to Marsh opening the subject, "but like many other chaps, I'm sure, I find it hard to keep my eyes off her, and imagine that the sort of night she would be good for, if she cared, would be a rare and lively experience!"

"She's been in Kashmir, here or Srinagar, for about three years, but has family connections she visits, in Lahore I think it is. Before that she was in Bombay Presidency, married to a chap in the I.F.S. where he was well up the tree, if you'll ignore the pun!"

"Lots of rumours went round about her, connected

with strange stories which have never had any sure corroboration."

"She gets on well with anyone who meets her, but seems to have no particularly close friends, much less any favoured suitor. Bachelor Army chaps from the host of subalterns and above on short leave return literally empty handed as far as she is concerned. People think she is merely waiting out the War here before going home for good."

"Nonetheless, there is enough of the sinister about Lucille Lansdowne to let her be as she is and not try to get involved with her, according to those who think they know."

"The basis of this goes back several years when her husband died rather inexplicably on the first of his forest inspection tours in the Eastern Circle of the Central Provinces just after he had been moved from Nasik. Lucille went with him as she often did - they had no children."

"He was said to have been killed by either a tiger or a panther, but villagers said that there was no tiger or tigress known to be in that or any adjoining forest block, much less a man-eater. John Lansdowne was a keen shikari and by virtue of his position naturally had access to all the 'khabbar,' or information, particularly of the larger carnivores, that the villagers and jungle dwellers in his territory were able to give him.

"The accident, if such it was, evidently happened at night. The khansama at the bungalow was asleep and the three forest Rangers Lansdowne had with him had gone off to the nearest jungle village for a toddy party. It was they who found him, horribly mauled, when they returned near dawn, but most of this had been the result of a visit from a pair of hyenas which ran off as they approached, followed by a male jackal. This fact would put the time of death as several hours earlier, probably before midnight. As for Mrs Lansdowne, according to her, she didn't miss her husband who was occupying a separate bed under his mosquito net, and she did not know anything until woken by the Rangers. This is not unlikely, as to see if someone is still in bed under a mosquito net is not that easy, you will agree. But Lansdowne was fully clothed. Lucille explained this by saying that she had gone to bed early, leaving him to write up his report; a perfectly normal situation."

Hamilton paused to light up a cheroot and ask for coffee to be brought to the table, while Richard settled himself to hear more of the story.

"Mrs Lansdowne," Hamilton continued, "is evidently one of those people, less usual in a woman, who don't go in for aimless chatter and whose emotions are not of the brittle or superficial kind. One wonders what her reaction will have been when the Rangers brought her husband's body in. One thing is sure, and that is that she would not have broken down or lost her self-control in front of the sort of companions she had at the time. She had been out in India long enough to feel, as memsahibs in her position do, that she had a strong image to keep up.

"All the same, the mangled state of her husband's body, with not another European within miles to share the shock, and at such an hour in the morning, would make a terrible impact on anyone. The fact was that when she returned to her bungalow in Nagpur she neither lost her self-control nor was in the least bit incoherent about the occurrence, according to what I heard."

"This all served her well at the subsequent post mortem and legal proceedings. The witnesses gave their evidence in the stolid way of Mahrattas, and it was not in the order of things to grill so unlikely a suspect as the victim's wife."

"I remember it now," Marsh cut in. "It didn't get much coverage in the Bombay Press. People were bothered at the bad news of the sinking of 'The Prince of Wales' and 'The Repulse,' and other reverses in the War with Japan, besides hearing firsthand about atrocities from wives and others who had got away from Singapore, Sumatra, and Java."

"People have talked about it more up here," said Hamilton "particularly when Mrs Lansdowne became part of the community, and it does seem that some questions will never be answered. In my case, being in the Government, I have heard the IFS people talking, and naturally, they were more than usually interested in analysing the circumstances.

"John Lansdowne had a severe head injury which could have killed him. A heavy fall could have done it. A tiger can be ruled out as as I said earlier. A panther would be unlikely to attack a human in the jungle unprovoked. The village itself would be a much more usual target for a bold animal in search of pi-dogs under cover of darkness."

"Lansdowne's limbs had been torn at, but the predators would have done this, including the fact that he was disembowelled. It is well known that a deaf and sleeping sloth bear will strike at the abdomen if disturbed, more usually in the heat of the day, while similar injuries are the common result of a wild boar attacking its victim on the ground."

"This sounds a faint possibility, despite the damage done by the hyenas and jackal, while the dust and drag marks they stirred up eliminated any other pugmarks the Rangers might have been able to identify, though it could be seen that pig often passed that way from nearby paddy fields."

"The usual cause of accidental death in the jungle is when some over enthusiastic hunter follows up a wounded dangerous beast too soon, isn't it? But what was John Lansdowne doing? He was not armed, and wasn't even carrying a flashlight."

"The thought does linger. Does Lucille Lansdowne know more of what went on that night, or, if so, was such knowledge so irrelevant to the tragedy that not keeping it to herself could not possibly have done any good?"

"What do you think about it, Marsh?"

"I couldn't say," Richard replied, "but it seems to me there is less harm in Mrs Lansdowne keeping whatever secrets she might have than giving way to idle curiosity. She may not have anything to live down, but your story makes sense of the feeling I got when I met her earlier tonight, which was one of decided fascination, yet tinged with wariness. She was not at all perfunctory, nor merely polite. Perhaps being firm with herself might describe it better."

Richard Marsh, at 27, was, in fact, good to look at. Tall, medium blond, and strongly built, with manly features and a frank demeanour. The kind of person people felt they could confide in, and be listened to. A good man to be in India, or anywhere else that native people could look to him for sympathy and guidance.

He should well have been with the Indian Army in Burma. He had easily passed the medical tests for call-up, but because the Indian Auxiliary Force in Bombay, which he still turned out with guarding pipelines and communication centres, had not been embodied as it had in Calcutta, and his business, already much depleted of younger Europeans and lack of new blood, needed him, he was classified 'Essential to Industry' and stayed where he was for the duration of the War.

He was used to it now. It meant a lot of long hours and lack of contemporary bachelor company as, one by one, his friends left for Officer training, but those he saw back from time to time had assured him that he was, often enough, doing more for the War effort than they seemed to be.

Having come this far on a long deferred bit of leave, and with his time running out, Richard wanted to see more of the country and wildlife if he could. Perhaps get hold of a tent and trek up one of the valleys then climb for a few hours in the hope of seeing Thar or Markhor and black, or even brown, Bear, besides smaller mammals and different birds.

A couple of days later, after he had dined on his own, one of the men he had noticed sitting with Mrs Lansdowne on his second evening in Gulmarg, came up and asked if he were alone would he like to join them for coffee. He nodded towards a table in the lounge where Mrs Lansdowne and one of the other men were seated.

Marsh readily agreed. He knew he'd like to have the chance to form his own opinion of Mrs Lansdowne after hearing Hamilton's story about her.

The man introduced himself as Arthur Hodge, and the

other man as Major Russell.

"I believe you have met Lucille Lansdowne?" he said, and they both smiled and nodded assent.

Hodge seemed to have been in the Indian Police, and evidently the two men, from their conversation, both had something to do with similar roles in Kashmir.

"So what have you found to do here since I saw you the other evening, Mr Marsh?" asked Mrs Lansdowne.

"Not very much, really," Marsh replied, feeling again that he was coming under the extraordinary spell of this woman, "but I haven't got much longer, so I thought I'd get out in the wilds for a couple of nights, probably hire a tent."

"You might be in luck," she said, "Arthur's going out to visit a couple of villages, complaining about bears killing their cattle as soon as they let them out, aren't you Arthur?"

Hodge agreed. "This always happens," he said, "mainly the black bears. They hibernate part of the winter, and naturally get hungry, but the villagers can't wait to put their animals out to the fresh pasture, and for the bears they are easy victims."

"But I didn't know bears were carnivorous," said Richard, in a half question, half statement.

"They are not, strictly speaking, are they Arthur?" asked Mrs Lansdowne sympathetically.

"Depends on the time of the year," Hodge replied. "Just now they go a bit mad. They will kill a cow, take a few bites out of it and leave it. Furthermore, it's not wise, Mr Marsh, to go camping alone. These are big brutes and not that afraid of man. By all means come along with us. Lucille and the Major will be there too. Day after tomorrow, early."

Lucille Lansdowne seemed all smiles and friendliness as the others got up to go, after Marsh, delighted at this unexpected invitation, hastened to accept it, and thanked Mr Hodge profusely.

"I suppose you are in one of the Club cabins?" she asked Marsh, "a bit primitive, aren't they?"

Richard wondered what was coming next. "Oh, mine is good enough," he said, "and I love to hear and smell the pines and deodars after the sal and teak forests and fleshy trees of the low lying jungles. It's like Switzerland."

"I know them well," she said. "Anyhow, come and have a nightcap in my chalêt, it's just behind here. The floor is well rugged and the fire should be glowing now. The servants make sure of their comfort the moment I am gone. I'll tell you about the expedition and what to bring. Not much, actually, Arthur likes his comforts."

Marsh hesitated, then reminding himself about taking people as one finds them, and glad to get a bit of advice, prepared to get up. "I'd like to," he said.

Mrs Lansdowne's hand went to a hard object in her handbag and produced a flashlight. Marsh smiled inwardly, thinking of Hamilton's closing remarks. Being alone with Lucille Lansdowne was certainly something to fire his imagination now, quite apart from her lovely features and perfectly carried junoesque female body. He thought of Rider Haggard's 'She,' who had been a sort of anti-heroine to him in his childhood. She had to be in some exotic setting. He could not imagine her at home in the atmosphere of suburbia.

Her living room was furnished in the style of a hunting lodge, yet not devoid of feminine touches. Richard thought that to be in such a place with such company positively spelt intrigue.

She offered him coffee and liqueur brandy, and he tried to settle down calmly in his leather armchair with it, one leg crossed over his knee.

"I think you are a lover of wildlife as I am, Mr Marsh?" she asked. "Though you may have heard that I have reason to be otherwise?"

"To answer your first question, Yes." said Richard. "India to me is a gorgeous storehouse of places accessible to all kinds of natural history. I don't know what I should have done in an office throughout these War years if I had not been able to pass many weekends out in the jungle. Secondly, Yes, I did hear you lost your husband in a jungle accident, and now that I have met you, I can see how you came through it, and are still content to be in this sort of atmosphere."

"I love the challenge large open spaces offer, and because of my husband's job I learned much about the ways of the wild. I would have gone crazy in memsahibs' parlours."

She put another log on the fire, and Marsh, watching her sinuous elegant movements thought of the easy grace of a panther.

There would be no flirtatious approaches from this woman, he reflected. You would find yourself suddenly and inexorably compelled to fling your arms around her, and what would your reception be? No better than that of some ardent, callow and sex-starved Army subaltern convinced that all solitary hill station wives were the same.

While Lucille Lansdowne described the needs for the forthcoming camping trip, Marsh sat wedged in his armchair, and when he rose to go he almost expected to hear himself come out of it with a plop like a cork from a bottle.

He said, "Goodnight, Mrs Lansdowne, and thanks so much, and for the coffee and brandy."

It was noteworthy that Mrs Lansdowne had never said, "Call me Lucille." He would have been surprised if she had, and even disillusioned. A strange feeling.

There were two bearers, a cook, a syce with two horses, and a Police sepoy, plus three local 'Admis' (village men) with two donkeys carrying one large and three small tents, food-stores, cooking utensils, and other small equipment. Mr Hodge and the Major who carried shotguns handed Marsh another one with some No. 6 cartridges and some buckshot. Mrs Lansdowne had a little .410 shotgun. She was all in khaki, slacks, shirt and Gurkha type puggareed hat. She looked businesslike and entirely at home.

They headed out along a beautiful valley blanketed up to the trees with wild flowers of every hue, and wherever it was damper, the small brilliant irises, emblems of Kashmir, nodded in unison in what little breeze there was. Richard was entranced. The air, not at all cold, was yet enlivened by the pure draughts coming from the snow-capped mountain slopes.

Every form of wildlife, mostly birds, that Marsh had seen on the golf course, was multiplied and added to by more species, particularly pheasants and chukor partridges, of which a number were later to be shot for the pot.

Marmots, their skins such a boon to mountain dwellers, abounded, besides other ground animals, many mongooses and weasel-like scurrying things.

The first village they entered was just as Mr Hodge had

said. The headman and others took them off to see a cow
that had not returned with the herd two nights before. It
lay dead, probably from shock as there was only one sign
of injury, a deep gash, about eight inches square on its
back behind the shoulders, the most tender part that one
might call the undercut. The bone of its spine was
visible and a huge chunk of meat had gone, simply
scooped out. Nothing more. Marsh was amazed. "A
black bear all right," said Major Russell, "typical."

Obviously there was nothing they could do about it.
All the headman wanted was to bemoan the loss and get
expressions of sympathy and, if possible, monetary
compensation. They all sat down and talked in a
language Marsh could not understand, a kind of pushtu.
Lucille Lansdowne remained apart, and got the porters
to shoo off the persistent village children.

"At least they don't ask openly for 'Baksheesh," she
said, approvingly, to Richard. "Come and see if we can
spot any thar or markhor through my glasses. They will
be ages yet before we can go on and get our camp set up."

A bit tongue-tied, Richard fell into step with her, but it
didn't matter as she went off like a denizen of the slopes
herself, evidently making for a tall isolated outcrop of
rock.

She pointed to it. "I've tried from there before, it
makes a good lookout as it is clear of the trees."

"Any luck, Lucille?" Richard ventured, looking at her
flat heeled leather shoes and his own thinner plimsolls.

Lucille Lansdowne didn't noticeably change her
expression, but something about the set of her shoulders
altered.

"All I saw last time was the tail end of a thar," she said.
"We must keep very quiet, even at this distance." She

followed a track through the trees with smooth strides. Richard kept just behind.

They were lucky as, on peering over the top of the rocky outcrop, three brown shapes of two of the adult goat-antelopes and one young one could easily be picked out moving slowly along a ledge perhaps 200 yards away. Through the glasses Richard could catch their every detail.

"Well, good, there you are," said Lucille, "but if you want to see a markhor, that's another thing. You'll have to go much higher than this now that the snow is melting fast."

"I think I'll try and organise a proper trek into Ladakh one day," Richard said. "With all the proper permissions and licences. The other thing I'll have a go at seeing, deviating a bit, is 'Barasingha,' the swamp deer. Is it true that the stags always have exactly twelve tines to their antlers?"

"Normally, yes, I believe so. Variations are a deformity really." She did not sound enthusiastic. "They are getting rare enough, as is the Kashmir stag also. I don't like to hear about people going out to try and shoot them in the Terai where they mostly are."

Richard felt that he wanted to put the matter straight. "I can't say that I am really mad about trophies," he said, "only to the extent that they are unique reminders of experiences and adventures on special occasions in wild and beautiful places. In my case they are only likely to be very few."

"Yes, I suppose there is some point in that," Lucille replied. "It is just that I love to see the four-footed beasts of the hills and jungles of India, and fear for their future the way so-called sportsmen use motor vehicles and high powered rifles with telescopic sights these days. I had more than a taste of this when I was with my late husband. I like to use a shotgun on game birds myself. This needs all the skill and junglecraft one can acquire and is not destructive."

Realising that this conversation rather changed his impression of Lucille Lansdowne, Richard kept silent as they turned and hurried back down, and watched his step as she displayed equal agility avoiding the steep bits of path with loose pebbles, and ducking under low branches, as she had climbing the rocky outcrop. Luckily, he managed to keep his footing.

The timing was good. They saw the bearers and porters heading along the valley and Arthur Hodge and Major Russell were about to salaam and take their leave of the village elders.

Camp was set up in a moss grown wooded hollow by a stream, full and cold from melting snows far above. Flowers grew everywhere on the approach.

The night was not as cold as Richard expected. The place was full of shadows when he awoke, roused by sounds from the kitchen area. He undid the tent flaps and looked out. He saw Mrs Lansdowne seated, with a rug over her shoulders, on a fallen log by the side of the stream about 60 or 70 yards away, apparently motionless. He drew back inside under his blankets. He woke up again half an hour later when a bearer brought him 'Chota hazri.' He lay, sipping the tea and thought again about Lucille Lansdowne.

Two things; she was a woman, and also an unusual person. Women, especially as fascinating as she, excited much individual interest or analysis at this time in India, because there were not many of them about. Even a plain woman with good qualities would have these and any other assets well recognised, better than if there was a wider choice based on looks alone. Mrs Lansdowne, however, thought Richard, was a worthwhile study in any circumstances. With a woman so independent there had to be a key which would open the door into a sharing relationship, fulfilling to both, which a man could enter.

He got no nearer to any enlightenment in the three days that followed. It was not like being within four walls. Each day the scenery changed, and became more magnificent, while the two other men quite belied Richard's Club member first impression of them. They even looked different, and fitted well into the surroundings of which, when it came to that, they had often enough been a part, and they were able to enliven the evening leisure hours with some good stories and anecdotes.

Lucille Lansdowne at times looked animated and knowing, and seemed on the point of adding some experiences of her own, but then it was as if she had to pull herself up as a shadow crossed her face, and she settled back in her camp chair once more just to listen.

After three days they turned back to their first camp where the villagers seemed satisfied with the attention they had received earlier, and by lunch time next day they were back in Gulmarg where Richard knew he had little time more than to say goodbye to Col. Dixon and one or two new friends and pack up for the long journey home to Bombay.

The War with Japan was over, and troopships to Europe were coming and going. Richard was expecting his time to be able to board one of them to arrive before long and could hardly keep his thoughts on anything else when a letter came from Gerald Hamilton in Srinagar.

"You will be sorry to hear," he wrote, "that, quite extraordinarily really, Mrs Lansdowne has been found dead from gunshot wounds in the chest, in the woods between Gulmarg and Srinagar. She had gone out looking for green pigeon and other small stuff and didn't come back. They found her the next day near where shots had been heard. No question of foul play. It is assumed she tripped clambering up a slope with the gun loaded, it was a 12-bore, but inevitably there has been talk of suicide."

Richard felt a flush come over him. No one who, like he, had seen Lucille Lansdowne move over rough ground and overgrown tracks could imagine her tripping, nor, at worst, leaving the safety catch off her gun.

He thought too, of her thinly disguised revulsion over people shooting at animals on the ground, and he had a sudden vision of a dark jungle slope somewhere in the region of Ellichpur with the body of her big game hunting husband lying there.

# MANGO SHOWERS

I was lucky enough to arrive in India at the start of the Cold Weather. I was proud and excited to be there. No clouds of World War II had yet gathered. No serious challenge to British rule was in the air and I had entered the most exclusive community in the whole of the British Empire, my standing assured.

More in India than anywhere else, probably because of the 'lingua franca' of Hindustani of which all Europeans needed something more than a smattering, a vocabulary of borrowed words and phrases after coming to the country to stay conferred upon users the recognisable stamp of membership of a unique society. Most implied some slight knowledge of the native language, but not all, others had to do, as in many other parts of the world, with local peculiarities.

I had heard of, but never seen, a mango before I came to India. One of my colleagues at the office, a fellow named Johnson, said to me as my first hot and sunny Christmas approached: "You're sure to get a 'Dollie' of fruit, if not several, from our agents, Alan."

Sure enough, we were working on the morning of Christmas Eve and when I arrived at the office there was the Pathan chowkidar guarding a cluster of tall round open work baskets full up with fruit and adorned with ribbon and a card bearing the names of the donor and the recipient.

"Apna wasti, sahib – this one is for you," said the chowkidar, indicating a good sized basket which he then took over to my car.

Two or three hours later, when enough work had been done and I opened the car to get in, the powerful odour of mangoes was the most sensuous thing imaginable. I hurried home as quickly as I could and put the dollie containing a dozen or more Alfonso mangoes, as well as sweet limes, large tangerine type oranges, chicoos, guavas – adding to the aroma – and a huge pomelo, into the shade of the kitchen for our Goanese cook to sort out for us later.

As a matter of fact I found meals, more particularly dinner, really something of a ceremonial. I was the fourth member of a chummery in a two storey bungalow of quite impressive size and appearance.

Each of us had our own bearer, of course, the other servants being common to the establishment. At meals, each bearer stood behind the chair of his sahib round the dining table and attended to his every need. The bearers, in white frock length jackets over their trousers, wound on a white puggree for the occasion as well as a wide cummerbund, and if their masters were in some army unit of the Auxiliary Force (India), as two of the chaps were, the bearer would be wearing the Regimental colours in the form of a sash round the waist and a narrower strip through his puggree, secured in front by a badge.

The mangoes came up for dessert. I stared at mine, and the fellow opposite, Maurice Dempster, demonstrated.

"These mangoes you got, Alan," he said, "are the best in India and probably the best in the world, not only because of their taste and colour, but they are so easy to handle. Look!"

Maurice took his knife and cut round the Mango's waist as one would halve an orange, until he felt the point of his knife against the stone. Then he picked it up in both hands and slowly twisted it round. It came apart easily, one half like a cup, which he put down, and then he eased the stone out of the other half with a fork. There was very little fibre left clinging to it.

"So, you eat these two halves with a teaspoon," Maurice said. "Then you can suck the stone. Nothing wasted, but be careful because mango stains are the very devil. These are called Alfonsos, probably by the Portuguese after their first King as they only grow around Ratnagiri down the Malabar coast near Goa."

They did seem rather rich, but there continued to be plenty of mangoes in the markets, getting bigger and better, and I could not resist their delicious taste.

The days began to get uncomfortably hot though the skies became more clouded over. Probably it only seemed so because of the soaring humidity, but soon I began to itch terribly from neck to shoulder blades. I had got prickly heat. People said it was good to get a suntan and swallow salt tablets. I did both of these things, and maybe I got off lighter than some.

Easter was going to be later this year, almost mid-April. The weekend before, Maurice and I were lounging on the first floor verandah after a heavy Sunday tiffin. Maurice looked up at the sky, mopped round his neck and cursed.

"There ought to be a few mango showers starting before too long now," he said.

"Mango showers?" I was visualising the fruit thumping down from the trees.

"Oh, yes, they are called that because they come off and on before the monsoon starts, and this is the time when mangoes are in full season."

I liked the name, but just to see the showers spattering on the city streets did not sound very inspiring. On impulse, I decided to get a coasting steamer to Ratnagiri and see if I could then go on somehow to Goa and get back on Easter Monday or early the next day.

Luck was with me. It could be done. I embarked on the SS 'Hirawati' (580 tons) of the Bombay Steam Navigation Company at 9.30 am on Good Friday, and hired a deck chair. Ratnagiri was the first port of call and we got there at 8.30 pm, and it immediately became obvious that the mango season was in full swing. Even at that hour I had to pick my way between boxes of the fruit practically covering the dock. Coolies were shouting and gesticulating and milling around as they got ready to load a quantity on to the boat.

I had been torn between getting off or going on to Goa because among the three other first class passengers there was a young and beautiful Portuguese senhora who, at that moment, was waving to me from the boat deck.

We had been sitting in our deck chairs all that afternoon, and then had tea together in the tiny saloon. I told her my name was Alan Fordyce.

"Mine is far to long," she said in good English. "Teresa Maria Dolodora de Gonzalez de Punto Basto. That's my husband's name at the end, but Teresa is enough. What are you doing here, Mr Fordyce?"

Her accent delighted me as much as her appearance. She seemed about 24, my own age or thereabouts I thought.

I told her about the Mango showers.

"I want to go and see them falling refreshingly among the jungle trees, and particularly in the mango plantations," I said, feeling a little foolish.

But I need not have worried. "I know about it," said

Teresa. "The Mango showers are like a warning to the growers. They know that if they wait too long, and the real monsoon rains set in their mangoes will be falling down on the ground." She turned a sweet smile on me.

"I never thought that I would find anyone like you out here, Teresa," I said. "How long have you been in India?"

"I came straight to Goa since one year with my husband, and he is an Agricultural official – is that right? He has had to go to Delhi for a conference, and I went to Bombay to have my teeth done."

There is something natural about Continental girls. They don't seem so stiff as in England, and more feminine. I had all my summer holidays on the Continent that I could manage before coming to India, and I fell in love twice; once in Switzerland, and once in Portugal, funnily enough. I seem to fall in love easily, or perhaps it is the holiday atmosphere. However it is, I was doing it again by the time I left the boat at Ratnagiri. I have reservations about married women, but there are always exceptions and Teresa was one: elegant and charming in every way.

She gave me her address and telephone number in Panjim, and told me she would take me to Old Goa on Easter Sunday. I was not sure yet how I was going to continue my journey, but boats were frequent enough it seemed.

Pushing my way out of the docks through the mob, I found a tonga and asked the wallah to take me to a hotel, the only one used by Europeans it turned out, and neither bad nor pretentious.

I went to sleep thinking of the Latin beauty of Teresa and her flawless olive complexion while listening hopefully for the splash of heavy raindrops. There were none. The night was clear and windless.

Next morning, after they had made a very creditable attempt at providing me with an English breakfast, I left my bag at the Splendid Hotel and picked up a tonga, noticing with satisfaction that some rain clouds were gathering.

I intended to get away from the coastal coconut groves as far as to where the jungle took over the ground as it rose into foothills not very far eastwards.

The way led through encircling mango groves which was just what I wanted. I dismissed the tonga after driving through to where the track petered out, and then went on for about a mile on foot into the jungle proper, no longer very dense, and carpeted with fallen leaves in places to where they had swirled in the warm wind. I made for a clump of large trees which were obviously evergreen and formed a dark glade within their canopy. They had thick curling trunks and large leaves bigger than my hand. I decided that I would be well protected by climbing into one, and picked a restful looking spot easy to reach, but high enough up to afford a good all round view. As I looked upwards a sudden cool wind started the branches swaying, and stirred up the fallen leaves round my ankles. I clambered up into my chosen perch where I could draw my legs up and support my back, and went into a sort of daydream.

The wind dropped as suddenly as it had started, and all went quiet. Then the heavy drops of a Mango shower came down perpendicularly, plopping on to the outer leaves of my tree and sparkling in the re-emerging sun. By now, although a spectator, I had merged myself with the jungle.

A scratching sound started twenty feet below me. Some fat little brown birds, hardly distinguishable from the freshly dampened leaves, were foraging round among them. They were jungle spurfowl, about half a dozen of them, tasty looking morsels themselves.

I had the feeling that something else might be sharing my thoughts, and I pressed myself further into the angle of the tree trunk. Suddenly there was a flurry among the spurfowl as they flew up and alighted about fifty yards further away into the jungle.

Placed as I was, I could not look behind me, bit I caught a glimpse of a panther's amazingly bright coat as she, not a very large female I judged, changed course at the spurfowls' retreat. Then I could only see her tail held elegantly just above the ground almost like a rudder guiding her, but futilely, after the spurfowl which again took off as before and disappeared from my view.

I did not realise until I had been in India some years how lucky I was to see that little drama enacted.

I waited a bit longer through another short shower. Nothing else happened around me. The stage was empty except for the raindrops. After a careful look around I shinned down the tree and started on my way back passing through the mango groves. Sure enough the showers had dislodged some of the heavier fruit, and I pocketed a couple of large mangoes, hoping that they were not too badly bruised.

I certainly had not expected Teresa to be actually on the quay at Panjim when I got off the small vessel bound for Calicut, which I had managed to catch, but there she was.

"Hello, Alan, I hoped you might be on this boat," she said, "so I came to look."

I stared at her. She might have looked fresh and neatly

dressed on the 'Hirawati', but now she would not have been out of place on the Faubourg St. Honoré in Paris on an August day.

I took her extended hand as if it was a delicate blossom I felt so travel stained myself, but she seemed quite unperturbed.

"Panjim is only quite small," she said, "but I will take you to the Hotel Republica. It is nice and not expensive. That is my car over there."

It was ten o'clock in the evening. I was not hungry, but I was tired and hoped I could get a bath of some sort. Teresa stayed for a glass of Vinho Verde and said she would call round in the morning. I put my crumpled khaki shorts under the bed mattress after finding a bathroom up the corridor, and scrambled under the mosquito net.

I woke up soon after daylight and immediately began to think about Teresa. I think I look quite presentable, even more so at that time than now, but here was a beautiful young Portuguese woman who couldn't have been married for very long treating me as if I was the catch of the season. There must be an answer somewhere, I thought.

The sun was behind the hotel, and I sat on the front terrace a few steps up from what was evidently a main street. Apart from a few pokey bazaar-like shops and their occupants the atmosphere was quite different from anywhere I knew in British India. It was definitely Continental. The terraced rows of stucco buildings were mostly of no more than two storeys high and had small shaded portico balconies below which were bodegas, or larger stores and shops.

Policemen and other evident officials, some of them white, understandably wore uniforms quite different from those in Bombay. The Indian natives looked much the same in their dhotis, but the obvious Goanese Christians wore European clothes.

What struck me most of all was the elegance of the Europeans passing in cars and tongas, but quite a few doing their shopping on foot. The men looked well groomed, and the women decidedly in fashion.

I understood better then the way Teresa dressed, but when she got out of her car, a Ford two-seater with a dicky seat, she had on a pair of baggy trousers and a cotton interlock short-sleeved shirt which disclosed, as I had only suspected before, the presence of a pair of perfectly formed breasts. She picked up a light straw hat and put it over her gorgeous black hair.

She had not seen me yet, and my pulse raced as she came along the pavement towards the hotel. I tried to compose myself.

"Oh, Alan, hello, good morning," she said as she paused on the steps. "Was it all right at the hotel?"

"Absolutely," I croaked, my eyes never leaving her. "I slept, as we would say, like a log."

"A log?"

"Yes, a big tree trunk too heavy to lift up."

"There are some like that on the beach," said Teresa. "Will you like to go there? I have brought something for us to eat for lunch."

"Yes, I would," I said, but I haven't got anything to swim in."

"Oh no, it is too dangerous now that the monsoon is getting nearer. Bad currents and jellyfish and very poisonous sea-snakes. But we can do some wading."

We drove off and turned left out of the main street, crossed a bridge over the creek, following a rough road down the side of the estuary, and then swung off again and came upon palm fringed grass covered sandbanks bordering the open sea.

The beach seemed to extend for miles and was deserted except for the dug-out canoes of fishermen, some of them with an outrigger on one side. Stray buildings roughly built of palm matting and mud or clay, a few with signs of life around them, could just be seen above the dunes, evidently marking the edge of a fishing village.

I took off my shirt, safe enough in my protective tan, and we walked down to the water's edge, and surveyed the sea which was more brown than blue, but warm and soothing to paddle in. We came upon three or four nasty looking corpses.

"There they are, Alan. Ugh, sea-snakes!" said Teresa, shuddering and gripping my arm tightly."

Ugly they were, a beige colour, about eighteen inches long, fat in the middle tapering to a small mouth and a pointed tail very slightly webbed.

It was getting uncomfortably hot, so we sought the shade of a palm tree leaning half way to the ground at an angle of less than forty five degrees. A line of bushy shrubs between us and the sea cut down the humid breeze. Some peculiar looking fruits were hanging there. We sat on the grass and leant against a fallen tree trunk. A couple of small land crabs, looking quite hollow, scuttered off from underneath.

Teresa's arm went around me and she started stroking my neck and head. She lifted her lovely full lips to be kissed.

Any harshness in our surroundings melted away. We were on a tropical island together, anywhere in the South Seas. Her legs were over my knee. Her dark, sweet smelling hair cascaded over my face. If I was uncomfortable it was far from important.

She drew away and told me about herself, giving me a measure of relief.

"After I left my Convent school near Lisboa I went to England for a year to learn English," she recounted. "It was not very easy for me when I went back home to Portugal as my family were the old fashioned kind. I could not do anything very much on my own in case I got us a bad name.

"It was certain, me being the only daughter, that my parents were going to arrange a marriage for me, and several men they approved of came to call with flowers and that sort of thing. It was all so formal and awful after England.

"I did not like much any of my suitors, but Roberto was in the Foreign Service and back from Mozambique, so I thought I would at least see some of the world with him. He is more than 20 years older than me. His first wife died of fever in Africa. He is generous and gives me nice things, but we cannot really love each other. He is also very jealous of me, so I do not feel free."

Of course I had heard of these sort of marriages in Latin countries, and I supposed that an Englishman like me turning up awoke in Teresa something that she knew she was missing badly.

Swept off my feet though I was, I forced myself to think rationally about my situation even though I knew that what was happening to us both was something that I would never be able to forget nor likely find again.

It had got too hot for us to stay on the beach, not being able to swim. I got up and went to look at the bushes in front of us, and examined the strange green fruit like a small pear with a pronounced hook the size of my little finger attached to the bottom of it.

I felt Teresa's closeness, and her hand on my shoulder. "Cashew nuts, Alan," she said. "Do not bite it. These hooky bits are the nut and they have to be dried for a long time before they can be eaten."

I picked a whole one off. "Is this poisonous or something now?" I asked, turning it over in my hand.

"No," Teresa tightened her lips hard. "Your mouth would go like this. Horrible, and very bad taste."

I slipped the fruit into my pocket, deciding to cut it open later.

She pulled down my head and kissed me. "Now we must go and see Old Goa," she said. "There we can have our lunch among the trees of a park, or in the shade of an old building perhaps."

We went back to the car, and seated, she threw her arms around me. Thank God we had left the windows open. Even then, as desire again welled up in me, the heat cut short our embrace.

I subsided into my seat, trying to use the odour of Teresa's body and her perfume as a narcotic as we wound our way back to the river estuary. As we passed the Panjim dock, the 'Hirawati' was there again discharging a cargo of tiles and domestic pottery from Mangalore. I said nothing on seeing it, but looking sideways, I saw tears in Teresa's eyes and swore under my breath. What irony, I thought, to win such a love, yet to lose it so inevitably.

We drove along the banks of the Mandvi river, so

silted up that little more than a channel of muddy water remained, and I understood why Old Goa, seven miles on, had relapsed back into the jungle.

Teresa was silent, watching the road for pi-dogs and scampering piglets, and I simply enjoyed being at her side watching the changing scene. She drove unhurriedly as we passed through two fishing villages and numerous palm groves. The dust was red and the road, walls and hillside were red, adding an artistic note to our route and lessening the glare.

As we neared Old Goa the road took the shape of a long boulevard with a high red wall on the right hand, inland, side. The dwellings here years ago, I thought, must have been those of the Portuguese grandee merchants, in their silks and satins, with their ladies, some of whom may have looked a bit like the one by my side.

Of the magnificent villas of the ancient capital only a few odd crumbling walls seemed to remain as far as I could see, enveloped in a palm forest and supplanted by a few native mud huts.

I spoke my thoughts to Teresa. "Don't you feel it is all very sad and ghostly?" I asked.

"Yes, I do, although I have been here many times I still think of how it was once more important than Bombay was, with rich Colonial merchants living here and watching the trading ships coming right up the river."

Paving stones at the end of the boulevard showed that we were reaching what was once a large square. A few partly restored houses could be seen between the walls of several larger ecclesiastical buildings. From one, the Cathedral of old Goa evidently, came the faint strains of organ music indicating that an Easter service was still in progress.

Teresa drove the car slowly into the shade of a beautiful viceregal arch. "This was built in the year 1512," she told me. "Imagine the important people landing here, Alan."

I looked through down the bank of the muddy river lapped by a feeble tide. An overgrown ferry stage and a small flat grounded boat were all that remained to be seen.

Teresa handed me a narrow straw basket. "Please, Alan, get this wet in the water down there."

"But it looks very muddy," I said.

"It's all right, it just has to be really wet."

When I brought the dripping basket back, she put a bottle of red wine in it and hung it on the low branch of a banyan tree. It started swaying in the warm breeze.

Several large stone blocks under the tree had obviously been used before by picnickers. Teresa brushed off one and put a rug over it. We were both hungry and soon finished off the lunch she had prepared. The heat in the car that the wine had taken on left it amazingly quickly as the dampness evaporated from the straw container.

We spread the rug on the ground and leant back against our stone seat. Teresa's kisses were on my cheek and neck. I felt drowsy as I watched the congregation dispersing out of the Cathedral away across the overgrown maidan and literally being swallowed up round the ragged corners of ancient buildings.

It seemed to me that we both dozed off, but when I awoke Teresa had gone and I found the traces of our picnic put back in the car.

She can only have gone across to the tall majestic church buildings, I reckoned, and I set off to what I had most wanted to see, the Church of Bom Jesus, resting place of St. Francis Xavier.

Inside it was dark by contrast and astonishingly cool. I walked along the side of the nave, and in a side-chapel saw a kneeling figure which I knew was Teresa. She turned her head round as I stood, and beckoned to me. I knelt beside her, not knowing quite what to do. She clasped my hand and I composed a prayer of my own. I suppose I asked a blessing for us both and thanked God for our meeting, and the present happiness of its outcome. I tried not to imagine further.

We got up and moved on towards the reredos where she pointed out to me the solid silver coffin of St. Francis.

"You found my note?" she asked me.

"No, I didn't see anything."

"Oh, I put it by your feet. It must have blown away. How did you know that I would be here?"

"I just thought you couldn't be anywhere else," I said, "and I wanted to explore round this part anyhow."

"Alan, amor, I am Catolica and we have Confession. I went to make one of my own, guilty perhaps, but so happy to find the love I want and to give thanks for being with you even a little while." Her tears began again.

I felt a little embarrassed this time. I admit to being sentimental and I have read a few romantic novels, but no heroine I encountered in them could touch the feelings of this lovely girl, I thought.

Once we were outside again and Teresa took over as my guide her mood changed and she was radiant. I looked at her classical features lighting up and marvelled at her.

It was growing cooler. She took my hand as we walked

along past various old buildings set back off weed strewn pavements. A few people were coming out to start their evening 'paseo.'

"Oh, Alan, when I am inside a Church I think of my wedding. I wish it had been to-day and with you!" She pressed herself against me.

Although I was trying not to think about the boat, and making the most of every moment left, the impossibility of any sequel to all this had me stuck for an answer.

Teresa supplied it herself. "Our religion," she said bitterly. "It helps us so often, my people think, but it has rules, especially for women, which can cause terrible unhappiness."

"I know," I said, with more than enough feeling.

We crossed over and back to the car.

Once more at the Hotel Republica in Nova Goa Teresa had left me with awful suddenness. Her mood had changed to one of urgency it seemed, and as if she had only just thought of it she said, "Roberto is coming back. He may be home even now. Wait for me at Panjim dock, Alan." She cast an anxious glance around her.

"By the boat jetty at 9.30," was all I had time to say before she drove off.

I packed my few things; left my topee with them and wandered out, hatless, into the cooling street. It was 6 pm and music was coming from the Park. I went there and sat down among the gathering crowd to listen to the Band.

The 'Hirawati," loaded with her cargo, was anchored off shore and passengers were being shuttled aboard by two motor boats from the jetty. I only saw two boat deck passengers. It looked like being a relaxing overnight trip to Bombay.

People waiting for the boat were thinning out and I was getting a bit restive as I scanned the usual clustering crowd of sightseers and relatives of the lower deck passengers. Then, with her face shaded by the same straw hat, I saw Teresa pushing her way through towards me.

Something about her demeanour struck me as she drew nearer. Contrary to what I had expected, and almost feared, she seemed unemotional.

Freeing herself from the crush, she ran the last couple of yards to me. "Oh, Alan," she said, "I am sorry to be late. Roberto was home when I got back from Old Goa, and it has not been easy." Her eyes were defiant, and as she buried her face against my shoulder she felt quite rigid.

I bent to kiss her, but she would not be held in it and turned her head in, clinging to me. I saw it then, a reddish bruise across her left cheek, and I felt a surge of indignation. The generous, but jealous Roberto? I wondered, but decided instantly that I must leave the initiative to Teresa.

I am sure she knew that I had seen enough of her face, but she let go of me and half turned, ready to flee like a frightened animal. I sought relief by ensuring my place in the queue for the next boat.

Teresa's dark eyes showed her pain at that, but the parting was over.

"I will write, Alan, oh querido," she said.

"I will write to you too, of course, and send you the photos; I promise." I felt myself choking, and as I turned away she raised her arm once and was gone.

The humid heat is nearing its worst in Bombay by mid-May and I was not the only one feeling run down.

Several friends I met at the Gymkhana Club, and elsewhere, were suffering from boils and diarrhoea, including Maurice Dempster who said that mangoes were partly to blame. I, myself, felt ominous signs of prickly heat returning, and was coming out with spots on my face.

"Better take some Metatone tonic, Alan," Maurice said. "Most chaps do at this time. The blood gets too thin. Doesn't seem to affect women so much though. In fact, the heat is supposed to make them more lustful: thinner clothing and so on, I suppose. A bit ironic, isn't it?"

"Yes," I agreed, though not in my case, I thought, but I didn't say anything more. Nor have I, until now, about that Easter in Goa.

# BEAU, THE PEACOCK

Every man, woman and child knows about the peacock. Few houses have not got a coloured illustration of this beautiful bird somewhere in a bookcase or drawer. Some may have a few of the wonderful tail feathers with their climbing bottle green fronds and brilliant blue, yes, peacock blue, eyes. What, too, does a rather gaudily dressed foppish young man do? He struts like a peacock: he is a beau.

'Beau' was just one original peacock. He would be contemptuous of our ignorance about him, thinking of peacocks as sort of domesticated adornments roaming freer than most things round Zoos and on the lawns of, and approaches to, stately homes, even in public parks, but nevertheless elusive, disdainful and hard to catch.

We rather take these lovely birds for granted, but where, in fact, do they come from? Somewhere in the East? Probably no Eastern potentate, be he King, Mogul Emperor, Maharajah, Caliph, Sultan or Savant would not have peacocks to grace his gardens and terraces. How had they come there? In baskets, as eggs, driven, or on their own from surrounding jungles, calling their loud 'meows' to each other as they came?

A jungle bird? Yes, this is where Beau was born and lived and died, like all his natural kind. He first saw the light of day on the edge of a forest on the Deccan plateau of India.

Wherever he looked there was a sea of grass, for it was July, and the monsoon had been pouring rain from the skies for a month. Here was one of India's great protections for its wildlife. Nature itself declared the closed season for hunters and poachers simply by enlisting the monsoon which coincides with the breeding season, not only for peacocks and other birds, but for four-legged animals too; the sambar, the cheetal, or spotted deer, the four-horned antelope, the barking deer, and the little mouse deer. They all got the respite they needed. Even the plains-dwelling blackbuck evaded the stalking villagers crouching behind their unfeared bullock carts.

In just two or three weeks the monsoon changes the world. Pause, and you can almost see and hear the vegetation growing. Only the bunds containing the paddy fields, now awash with mud and water, and ready for planting out the rice, stop the march of growth. Reeds and grass more than head-high extend in a bowing wave to the jungle edge where it laps around the forest trees mingling with shooting saplings and other growth, and darkening all with the aid of the large leaves of sal and teak, and the thick clumps of bamboo. The jungle is left to itself as far as man is concerned for a full four months.

At least from man in any case, peacocks like Beau and his brothers and sisters had another safeguard, for in many districts of India they are held sacred.

His mother told him, when the time came, about the panther, the all year round menace to peacocks.

"You can run fast, very fast, my son," she said, "the ground is where you find your food and spend your days. Our hearing is not special, but we have the sharpest eyes in all the jungle. You will find this out, and, like us all, be too proud to take to your wings at only a hint of danger. But if it is real watch some of us adults, we can fly up like a rocket and away out of reach better than any jungle fowl or crow pheasant if we need to."

Beau learnt this one day when he was still small. He saw the tip of a ringed tail, and before the civet cat charged, a quick run and he was airborne. What an amazing feeling.

He would have had to fly soon anyway, because peacocks, like dark shadows, black when there is moonlight, spend their nights roosting well up in the trees and safe from prowlers. The Indian panther of the plains does not climb like his African leopard cousins.

When the monsoon was over, the late Summer heat returned, ripened the rice and scorched the grass and undergrowth, so that the forest glades cleared and the world opened up. The peacocks divided up into sizeable troops, and the males segregated themselves from the females after whom trotted Beau and others of his age. These pea-chicks, barely able to fly, learnt the use of their eyes as the distances lengthened.

The villagers came and harvested the rice as the water left the paddy fields, and soon, as the Cold Weather began, the foraging of wild boar shook out what husks remained, and a copious supply of grains of rice lay upon the ground.

This was the time of feasting for the peacocks who came down at dawn and called happily to one another as they fed. Beau's mother made sure that he and his brothers and sisters returned to the forest before the sun was well up, but the older ones lingered, greedily, longer. Then everyone came out a second time as the sun began to set and stayed until dark.

On this diet Beau grew rapidly, and his gathering colours soon distinguished him from his sisters in their brown coats, and no more than mufflers of bottle green. Soon he would join the older males in their lives of independence.

He saw his first close-ups of human beings as he became bolder and more sure of himself.

"They are not dangerous, the ones who live near us and use bullock carts, Beau," his mother had said. "In fact, they admire us, and make pictures, and even images of us, for their temples and homes. They tell stories of us and say we are chosen of the gods. But other men from towns come in fast motor cars, carrying guns, and they do not respect us and would dare to catch us to eat or sell."

"Since the Sahiblog left our country," she continued, "there are no fresh hunting laws in the land. The fair-skinned men in topees in these cars are Anglo-Indians, and they don't care in the same way for the jungle folk."

Beau saw something of this one day when, with a few friends, he followed some of the older birds out near the village. These had started scratching on the dust road when a motor car came fast round a corner. The peacocks saw it immediately, of course, and expected it to slow down, but instead, it went faster and hit one of them, which managed to fall into the nullah off the side of the road. The men got out of the car to pick up the unlucky bird, but they had been seen by some villagers. These set up a shout, and others came running, waving sticks and picking up stones. They would have belaboured the three men from the car, but these scrambled back in and drove off as the villagers dashed up and dented the back of it. Molesting, and worse, killing a peacock, was severely punishable where Beau lived. Even the grey langoor monkeys with their black faces, insulting the peacocks from the trees above, were sacred too. After all, they were once part of Hanuman's army.

Beau and his young friends were both warned and reassured by this event they had seen.

As the cool days continued, hunters came into the forest with their guns, well away from the villages. It was a bad time while it lasted. Beau learned that these guns could shoot a bird down while it was flying. The hunters hid and tried to make the peafowl fly up by suddenly surprising them. They could see them easily then, but if they stayed on the ground, the hunters had little chance of seeing more than a flash of colour as they made off on their strong legs through the undergrowth.

The cool weather gave way to the scorching heat of the true Hot Weather of April and May, and now the jungle grew dry and bare, leaves fell rustling to the ground to be blown away by the whirling of dust devils, miniature tornadoes. All the world was brown, and men came to check and clear the forest fire-breaks.

Brilliant splashes of red appeared on some leafless trees. These were the flowers of Flame of the Forest, Pink Coral and Silk Cotton trees, harbingers of the pre-monsoon heat, just as Cherry trees bloom before the Spring brings them their leaves.

Then, too, the glory of the peacocks' colours and train-tail grew to their finest and most brilliant. These colours bedecked Beau too, though his train needed another year to reach its full magnificence. Never, in any park or zoological garden, could a peacock appear in the full glory of these wild ones as they stood or moved before the backcloth of red-brown jungle.

A few hunters still came, but now there could be no surprise, and the peafowl always saw them first. Somehow, Beau observed, the peafowl, some hens now beginning to join in with the cocks, seemed, as he watched them from a thicket, to know just how far was beyond shotgun range, and he noted this instinctively for himself. The peafowl moved along defined paths, and they proceeded in single file. Once, two hunters, one a woman, came near, perhaps one hundred yards away. They were sahibs, pale and well dressed.

The peafowl had sensed them at double the distance and were not alarmed. They did not turn back or scatter, but fell into single file. Then, at about 80 yards they divided into two lines, one of only peacocks, and the other almost all peahens. The man raised his gun at the leading peacocks who, quite unhurriedly, widened the wedge between them and the peahens and proceeded to go round the hunters, always maintaining the same safe distance, as, also, did the hens.

As Beau watched, he saw the man lower his gun, smile and say something to his companion. The peacocks, perhaps about twenty of them, filled a clear space on the dusty brown path, each one almost beak to tail, their delicate crests nodding above vigilant eyes. No sight like this can be excelled in any of Nature's treasure houses. It was as if a shimmering blue necklace was threading its way along the parched jungle path.

The watching man put his arm round the woman and their eyes were shining in a way that said they could never have foreseen that their hunt would provide an experience so enchanting as that.

It was soon the time of the courtship of the peacocks, the time when the males would dance for one hen after another, spreading their tails into a gorgeous fan until at least one peahen was captivated with the beauty of it. Beau never saw a peacock without a mate at this time and was not quite sure which his own was until, sitting on her eggs, she commanded him to stand by just as his father had done a year ago, as the monsoon unleashed its sheets of rain and the grass grew green and tall again.

# ABU'S MOUNT

In the Dak bungalow's central room at the large table Jonathan Harris paused to grab the Flit gun and squirt some insecticide under the table and round his ankle socks, then rubbed some over his hands.

Thank goodness it is the Cold Weather he murmured to himself, directing a final shot at the hurricane lamp resting just clear of the paper in front of his left elbow.

Mosquitos were not much of a pest in January when wearing slacks and long-sleeved shirts or jerseys gave added protection.

After the predictable meal of chicken and caramel custard provided by the Khansama, and a pleasant smoke on the verandah, the job of keeping his reports up-to-date was vital or details of the day's work would fade.

Each day involved an inspection of a fresh cotton mill, a groundnut pressing factory for oilcake, or a sugar cane crushing shed for the juice, and the piling up of the spent cane for 'Bagasse' for its value as fuel.

Outside, the night sky was full of stars bright enough to cast purple shadows among the trees and nothing broke his concentration; only a faint sound of chatter came from the servants' quarters out at the back of the bungalow.

The place where Jonathan Harris found himself in the course of a 'Mofussil,' or up-country, tour of some of his Company's agencies, was a little way out of the capital town of the same name as the Indian State ruled over by the Maharaja Holkar of Indore, one of the three Mahratta principalities in Gujarat.

Of these States, feudal and mainly agricultural, of

which Baroda and Gwalior are the other two, Indore had the largest and most thriving business centre of the area and seemed to Harris to provide a central clearing house for cotton.

"We have also this very big State owned cloth market, Mr Harris," the Agent, Narendra Dalal, told him. "Many textile piece goods are daily going in and out."

Harris, reading over his report, felt glad that he had come. It began:-

> 'The reason for my visit to Indore was the receipt of instructions from Bombay stating that N.C, Dalal & Sons, our Agents, had written complaining of conditions of unfair competition, adding that a personal visit of an official was desirable.'

Day well spent, he thought. It was always the same breaking new ground. You started the day feeling lost in unfamiliarity, and wondering how best to achieve something. Then, in the reality of it all, things seemed to look less formidable, and ended by working out better than expected quite often. Indore had been like that.

He took up the paraffin lamp and went through the sleeping room, bare except for one clothes cupboard, a bed with mosquito net over a rectangular wooden frame, a bed-side table with another lamp on it, and several rush mats on the stone floor.

Beyond was the usual almost bare room serving as a bathroom, housing a zinc bath with a wash-away channel, beloved of snakes more than occasionally, that emptied itself outside through a hole in the wall.

A Victorian washstand with mirror and drawers, and two cane chairs completed the amenities. Being late, and growing cold, Harris decided not to go through the ritual of a bath until the morning.

More than ever at the end of a day like this, alone and with a job well done, Jon Harris gazing comfortably from his bed through the whiteness of the mosquito net, thought about Adela.

After setting sail for India from Tilbury, as had others before him, Jonathan had fallen in love on the ship coming out. The combination of the sights, sounds and atmosphere of the East, starting at Port Said, and the arrival on board there of a lovely and vivacious girl, made an irresistible recipe for romance. Adela Orde and a former school friend, with her mother, was on a world tour, an alternative to being presented at Court offered by her parents.

Jonathan pictured again the scene on his arrival in Bombay, 'Urbs Prima in Indis,' the gateway to India, and how, before being swallowed up in the milling crowd on Ballard Pier, he had turned, sadly, and just managed to see the figure of Adela waving her farewell from an upper deck of the ship. He had raised his arm in a gesture that was meant to be reassuring.

"Come along with me," his firm's accountant, Ivan Warner had said after a warm greeting. "Our office sepoys will see about your luggage now."

They got into Warner's car and threaded their way out of the docks. Overhead numbers of mewing black kites swirled around looking for scraps and driving off the less aggressive seagulls.

The central streets of the city were thronged with pedestrians, bicyclists and occasional hack victoria cabs forcing their way along.

Warner drove expertly, though with much use of the horn, cutting a swathe through the mass of white garments which parted just before contact like water flowing round a boulder, coming together again immediately behind the car.

"I suppose this is the rush hour?" Harris asked.

Warner nodded. "It always is."

Adela had gone to Calcutta by train later in the day. Jon was glad to be fully occupied, he remembered.

They had decided they wanted to marry, and agreed on a sort of provisional engagement during the waiting years. Adela had written from Peshawar, Agra, Colombo, Penang, Japan, Hawaii, and Banff in Canada.

Harris had been in India now for eighteen months and, sometime in November, Adela was definitely coming out to be with him for at least a month. How he hoped to be able to show her some of the India he had learnt about and actually know, such as this out of the way place.

He dropped off to sleep.

It was while Jonathan was on one of his tours that he had visited a Jain temple in Ahmedabad; a very beautiful and ornate shrine to the founder of Jainism, the Prince Mahavira, and more than twenty others believed to have brought the religion to the world.

Stories about Hindus to whom cows, monkeys, and peacocks were inviolate, and others who wouldn't hurt a fly, were told in England and these were the sort of things that Jonathan had wanted to know more about.

Most of the Europeans he got to know in Bombay made their own lives in the way of British colonials, relying on Clubs, sporting and social events, as well as hotels, cinemas, western style shops, and department stores for their recreation and needs.

For the majority of expatriates such things, highlighted by colourful hospitality at Government House and parties at Army or Navy venues, were sufficient.

Jonathan took time to read and learn what he could about the culture, religions and history of India which gave rise to its wonderful palaces, temples and monuments.

In this, he was helped by the chief clerk of his office, a venerable and learned man nearing retirement, who was known by all and sundry as Mr Shripad.

Mr Shripad was expert in mapping out tours, and Harris turned to him from the start to fill in the essentials of those he had made to Gujarat, Kathiawar, Rajputana, and the Central Provinces.

It was the Jains, he found out, who would not even crush an ant if they stuck to the letter of their faith, which taught that the life of even the meanest thing was precious.

The founder of Jainism was Nattaputta Vardhamana, born somewhere between 599 and 556 BC, the second son of the King of Mogadah, a small Kingdom in the north of India. He was actually a contemporary of Siddhartha Gautama, the Buddha, and their early lives followed a very similar pattern. Vardahamana, after a youthful exploit of bravery took on the title of Mahavira; the Great Hero.

Like the Buddha, Mahavira left his father's kingdom, and wandered the land as a monk preaching sermons which, as did Buddhism, sought changes in the ancient Hindu religion, particularly as regards castes and opposition to aspects of Brahmanism and dependence on the Hindu pantheon of Gods.

However, whereas the Buddha taught moderation and a realistic approach to life, Mahavira preached asceticism, a pure life, and even self-torture, and the vital importance of any form of life on earth.

"The first Commandment of Mahavira is: do not kill

any living thing, or hurt any living thing by word, thought or deed," Mr Shripad said, "this is called Ahimsa, and it means non injury to anything that has a soul. Mahatma Gandhi used it to support his policy of non-violent non-co-operation."

"But surely," Jonathan asked, "these rules and beliefs must be very hard to keep up, especially these days. How many followers of Jainism would you say there are?"

"Not many more than two million, I suppose," said Mr Shripad, "and of course, it could never become a world religion; less than ever now, because Jains are not permitted to till the soil for fear of killing worms, nor can they cut down trees, nor use furnaces for fear of burning flies and other insects. For all the necessities of life they have to depend on others, and they are of course, strict vegetarians."

"Then, really, it is just an idealistic sect," said Jonathan. "But what I don't understand is how did they get the money to build marvellous temples like the one I have seen in Ahmedabad?"

"Oh, yes, Mr Harris, because Jainas cannot be farmers, or soldiers or industrialists they are mostly merchants and bankers, and the wealthy ones among these built the temples to their founders. Have you heard of Mount Abu?"

"No, I haven't."

It is not far away from where my family comes, but it isn't in our office's territory. It is a small and beautiful hill station about 4500 feet high near the top of a mountain in the south of Rajputana."

"Mount Abu is the most sacred place in India for the Jainas who go there on pilgrimage to the Delwara Temples. These temples, of which there are five, many people consider to be the second wonder of architecture in India after the Taj Mahal."

Jonathan was thinking quickly. "Do you know, Mr Shripad, that my fiancée is coming to Bombay to see me for a month or so in November? What would it be like in Mount Abu then?"

"That is happy news, Mr Harris. November is not too hot, nor too cold, and everywhere the hills and trees and flowers will be best, after the monsoon rains."

Jonathan thanked him. "I will try and get ten days leave; don't tell anyone!"

Mr Shripad grinned: he liked young Mr Harris.

Like clockwork, storm clouds brought Jonathan to his second monsoon in the middle of June.

Instead of a sea of flowing white garments, the centre of Bombay was a forest of black umbrellas bobbing around tip to tip. Whatever could be recalled of the fair condition of the servants' umbrellas of the year before, a new one was always extracted.

Streets were awash and steam rose from them to make the visibility worse. Cars stalled and palm fronds detached themselves and crashed to the ground. Cotton stored in dock godowns with inadequate ramps got soaked when the clouds opened for days on end.

Nevertheless, the monsoon provided its own activities for Jonathan Harris and his friends. There was rugby football, squash rackets, and the so-called mud sports for horse riders.

Female company was at a premium. Wives who could spend a month or two at a Hill Station were absent. Maharaja's' winter palaces were vacated, and the Government, with its social round, transferred to Poona.

For Jonathan particularly, such things were not a deprivation. Adela's arrival time grew nearer.

Following his talks with Mr Shripad, he read up what

he could find about Mount Abu. Few people he knew had been there personally, and various small hill stations around the top of the Western Ghats where husbands could go for an occasional long weekend, were naturally favoured.

At Mount Abu, Jonathan reckoned that he and Adela could be comfortably incognito. It was not shown on any ordinary maps that he came across outside the Library, yet it was important enough to be the Residency of a Political Officer who, as Agent for the Governor General, or Viceroy of India, is the Government's representative in Rajputana.

It lies on a plateau of the southern escarpment of the Aravalli Hills, on another side of which is Udaipur, about 450 miles equidistant from Bombay and Delhi; has a lake and, apart from the Delwara Temples, there are numerous places holy to the Hindus.

The scenery, Jonathan read, was described as soft and romantic. Perfect, he thought.

Well, there's always a chance to save up in the more limited social activities during the monsoon, he said to himself, and what about an engagement ring? I'm going to do all I can to make this a wonderful half-way re-uniting until my first four years are up when, God willing, Adela and I can be married at home.

The way her letters had kept coming made Jonathan determined to get ready and make sure that everything was right at his end. He had already seen too many engagements founder because of long and distant separations.

Then a letter fell on his desk like a bombshell. "Jon darling," it said, "of course you know – from the very first moment I told you – that I was definitely coming out, and I am, and my parents agreed, but they have been asking some awkward questions.

"You see, I told them that I was going to stay with a girlfriend whose parents are in New Delhi, and I have had to make a proper story of it. I haven't told them about us, as they are hoping that I will do all the right things here and marry someone with a title. It's all right, but don't think of writing to my parents or anything like that. I am supposed to be getting all the arrangements going – after all, I'm 21 now – and fixing the dates and so forth.

"I love you awfully, and no-one will stop me . . ."

Jonathan had two reactions to this news. First was the awful sinking feeling, and next, one of indignation. He knew he wasn't, at the moment anyway, a great catch as a son-in-law, but when a man wants to make a girl his own and she agrees, he wants the whole world to know about it. To have to go through a process of establishing his credentials really was a bit galling, and his family background and education were most acceptable. Most employers went into that before sending people to India.

After sleeping on this setback, and grabbing the straw of Adela's clear intention to quell any opposition he decided not to give vent to his feelings and make matters worse.

Then, after a week, the cablegram came. Adela had booked her passages, to arrive on November 15th and leave on 2nd January. Mount Abu was going to be on.

The rains were over except for some lingering storms which refreshed the growing heat, Jonathan's leave was fixed for December 4th, and Adela had arrived.

He had arranged for her to board with his favourite young married couple, and they all took to each other.

As soon as he dared, Jonathan raised the subject of their engagement.

"If I had announced it," Adela said, "my parents would never have let me come out here you see, and that would have been the end. We could never have gone four years without seeing each other again, could we, Jon?"

Almost reluctantly, Jonathan had to agree.

"Yes, it's a terribly long time," he said."When we met like we did anything seemed possible, but these two years have seemed interminable. I think that if you hadn't come now different things could easily have happened to change us, inside and out, though your letters have been wonderful."

"So have yours, darling," Adela assured him, "but here we are, and I am thrilled at going to a hill station with you. It is almost exactly two years since Doris and I and her mother were on our way to Delhi and Agra."

"You never saw anything of Bombay then," Jonathan remarked, "and now the season is just starting. It's not difficult to borrow a horse for you for us to do some riding, and then there'll be weekends when we can go off in the car to some of my jungle haunts. There are plenty of parties and things too."

In countries like India where, in any young man's first few years there, it means living a bachelor life, to have an unattached female companion brings much more spice to it than can be imagined back home. Suddenly, from being little more than a bystander, Jonathan Harris had a girl entirely to himself, and Adela was even prettier than he remembered.

They were invited out a lot, and Jonathan basked in the limelight, conscious of envious, if not covetous, glances from his friends and others.

He hurried with Adela to choose an engagement ring, just to avoid any misunderstanding, and ready when the time came for their holiday to Mount Abu. Adela had found out some more about the place. "It takes its name from Hindu mythology," she related, and quoted from what she had read: "The town is on a plateau about twelve miles long and two and a half miles wide at the top of the Mount, where the landscape is at its charming best just after the rains."

"Now, in fact," said Jonathan.

"Don't interrupt, darling." Adela scolded, chuckling.

"Mount Abu is venerated by Hindus throughout India and is mentioned in the Mahabarat. Legend has it that the younger son of the mountain Himalaya, Nandi Vardhan, was sent there on the back of a serpent, an incarnation of the goddess Arbuda, and established it as the mountain Arbudachal which became shortened to Abu. It started by being a stronghold of the followers of Shiva, and later, the Jainas, and still is a place of pilgrimage for many Hindu sects."

"It also says," Adela went on, "that Abu has a bustling bazaar and a lovely lake about half a mile long and a quarter mile wide, the Nakhi Talao, said to have been excavated by the finger nails of the gods, and that a number of Rajput princes have summer palaces round its shore."

"Phew," exclaimed Jonathan. "You have done well, it doesn't look as if we're going to be bored, does it?"

"Hardly, not that we shall mind, darling. It seems really civilised. Apparently Mount Abu was within the State of the Maharao of Sirohi who let the British Government establish a Sanitarium there in 1845 for their soldiers stationed in India. Then after the first World War it was leased in perpetuity as part of British India."

"More importantly," said Jonathan, "I believe there is

a good hotel for us there?"

"Oh, yes, the Rajputana Hotel; for Europeans only, it said, with 34 rooms, double and single."

"I'll book it for us right away, Mr and Mrs" Jonathan grinned archly.

At last, for 4th December, they got their tickets on the B.B. & C.I. Railway's Delhi Express, changing at Ajmer the next morning, from where a branch line ran to Abu Road. Here the countryside is flat and plain-like but as they got out of the train the atmosphere was already dry and cooler.

There was no need to linger; a coolie collected their cases and bedding roll and trotted out of the station to where an office said: 'The Mount Abu Motor Service.' Six or seven people were queueing up at the counter inside.

Jonathan asked the clerk what the transport to Mount Abu was.

"You can reserve a touring car, but minimum three seats are charged, Sahib," the clerk said. These two ladies will make up four passengers with you which is maximum. Three more can go in next car."

"Fine for us, eh Adela?" Jonathan said, agreeing to the inclusive fare of 22 rupees with the others who turned out to be two Indian hospital nurses.

After going for about nine miles north west on a good road, they started up towards the mountain which rose abruptly and zig-zagged on through spectacular scenery and lush vegetation, crowding the sides of a long narrow and deep valley for another eight miles. Thin cascades of water splashed into ravines at the side of the road.

The going was very slow, but Adela and Jonathan spoke little, drinking it all in and revelling in the fresh colder air. After one and a half hours they arrived at the

Rajputana Hotel, driving through the lovely little town.

"What cute bazaars," Adela said, "it reminds me of an Italian village."

The hotel was less than half full and their accommodation was a spacious twin-bedded room with a lounge and two bathrooms leading off it.

After a wonderfully refreshing night's sleep they went out to explore, strolling down to the Nakhi Talao Lake. They took out a boat and rowed half way round one end. Later they bought a map and guide at the hotel, and after dinner, went upstairs to look at them. In the lounge a log fire was burning in the fireplace. Adela washed her hair, and they lay down together reading about things to see while she dried it in front of the fire.

One of the comfortable beds was just right for two together after that. Through the window the moon rose and illuminated the mountain crags high above the plateau.

They explored the bazaars which were full of exotic fruits and vegetables and things for picnicking. They both ordered shoes and slippers to be made, and Adela lingered happily over colourful dress materials.

Following paths out of the town there were many shrines and pilgrim spots along the way, and after this they decided to make plans to go to three special places for a full day out, taking picnic lunches.

First of all, Vashisthashram. Vashistha, they learned, was the great sage who had got help from Himalaya to found the mountain Arbudachal. He was also believed to have been the teacher of Rama.

They had to go two miles down the road that they had taken from Abu Road Station three days before.

"I hope this guide book is accurate, Jon," Adela said. "It didn't do too well in finding Sunset Point for us."

"Well, about here there should be a footpath where we evidently have to go down an incredible number of steps."

Then they found these, not too overgrown, and down they went through groves of mangoes and other beautiful trees with fragrant flowers, pausing often to inhale jasmine and balsam and other scented shrubs, while noting many shady stopping places for the climb back up later.

At the bottom was a well-built 'Tank' replenished continuously with cool clear water out of the mouth of a marble cow's head. This was Gaumukh, and above it ran a verandah and two small temples, while in front, within a courtyard, was Vashistha's Ashram and a temple with the image of the sage and his two famed pupils, Rama and Laxman, heroes of the Ramayana.

The tank was no more than three feet deep. They saw a man and a woman stepping out of it, so undressed behind a wall and bathed and sun-bathed delightedly.

Back in the courtyard Adela said, "What a lovely place for our picnic," and, as if he had heard her, a smiling old man in priestly garb came out of the Rest-house at one side. Adela showed him the food that they had brought, and Jonathan asked him in his fair hindustani if they could eat there.

"Ha-ji, achha hai, Memsahib," the priest said, placing his hands together and beckoning them under the pillars from where he proceeded to show them around. He then gave them a few succulent bananas.

"This lovely fellow must be the 'Mahant' who the book says looks after the temple," Jonathan said. Then with a self-satisfied smile, he added "Memsahib!"

"Some day maybe!" Adela replied.

Two days later they set off on their second excursion.

This was to find the temple of Arbuda Devi. Instead of down this time, it was round the Lake Nakhi Talao and up to the top of a hill north west of the town. Some of the way a path led them up over slopes leading, in some places, to flights of steps, often badly worn.

Although the going was rough at times, and the vegetation luxuriant, the many flowering shrubs made it a pleasure to stop and inhale their fragrance and, as they climbed, more views opened up of the lake and the plains spreading out beyond the Mount.

Nearing the summit they saw a white building with a low dome on the skyline.

"That must be the temple of the goddess," Adela said, pointing.

"Yes," Jonathan agreed, "we are pretty near now. Let's have our lunch there. I bet you're hungry. I am."

They came up to it and sat down to their picnic lunch thankfully, but noticed with disappointment that the temple did not have much adorning it, and none of the usual signs of offerings of flowers or scraps of food.

Just as they were finishing, a group of half a dozen pilgrims came up from a small path on their left and their leader greeted them in English.

"Have you been to the temple of Arbuda Devi?" he asked.

"Is this not it?" Jonathan queried.

"Oh no, Sahib," the man said. "This structure is to show the position. You must please to go down this path and you will find a little wooden door on the rock with carvings round it. The temple is there; it is very many years old."

They thanked him, and soon found the door which was the only entrance to a dark cave. They squeezed through and right opposite was the garlanded image of the Goddess. Guttering in niches of the wall were numerous little lamps, their wicks floating in ghee, evidently replenished from the pot which they had seen at the entrance. Burning tapers of incense completed a more ethereal atmosphere than any shrine the two had seen before.

Adela slipped out through the doorway and came back with some jasmine petals. "Some for each of us," she said, sprinkling hers at the feet of the statue. They threw their arms around each other, kissing with the passion the mystical twilight had aroused in them.

"Lord, I hope they never have electric light in here; seriously," Jonathan pleaded.

"Oh, darling, so do I." Adela's eyes were shining in the dim light.

They blinked in the sunlight outside. It had got very hot, but back on the summit a strong wind blew. They looked at their map and followed a line along the top to the south of the lake, then down a well-defined path which joined Bayley's Walk back into Abu town.

The Jain Temples at Delwara, a village only about a mile east of the town past the Sanitarium were to be their final goal.

Passes were needed to enter the temples, and these they were able to get at the Rajputana Hotel. The friendly proprietor, Mr Hormasji Framji, a Parsee, told them that it would be enough to go round just the two most wonderful temples, and he was right.

These were: the oldest, Adinathji, built in 1032, and Neminathji, built in 1231, both at enormous cost in materials and labour.

They could not have been more of a contrast than to Arbuda Devi's cave temple of two days before.

More exquisitely carved marble has been used in their

construction than any other temple or mausoleum in India excluding the Taj Mahal, which both Jonathan and Adela had seen, and could compare.

Of the two recommended by Mr Framji, Jonathan and Adela both chose Adinathji's Temple. Neither one was dedicated only to Mahavira, but to all the founders of Jainism who came before him, called Tirthankers, two of whose names were borne by these temples.

All the images inside were of the founders and some of their wives and families, and it was there that the full beauty and intricacy of the carving made Jon and Adela gasp.

Corridors flanked by rows of pillars supported dome-like porticos and central pendants as big as chandeliers, all carved in marble worked to perfection.

The fact also that the Jains do not ignore the Hindu gods of mythology was evident in ceiling paintings of their lives and exploits.

It took them two hours to get around and they came away quite dazed by it all, but there was still time left to go to the lake once more and swim and sun-bathe. Then to stroll through the bazaars as the sun went down.

Too soon next day the train took them on the journey back to Bombay's Victoria Terminus.

Christmas had come and gone, and New Year too, and a ship like the one that had brought them together bore Adela away.

Two days after, Jonathan, not to feel utterly desolate, had managed to arrange to make a short business tour, but before that, he had never known such sickness in his heart. It was worse than tears, which could help to wash away a sadness. Part of him had simply gone, numbing emotion and clouding his mind.

It would, of course, pass, and surely the magic of the moon on Nakhi Talao and the spell of Arbuda Devi's cave could not fail to bring them together again.

# THE SAUSAGE HUNT

I was sitting one evening on the lawn of the Royal Bombay Yacht Club, unpretentiously as befitted a new Member, when an older resident of the Bombay Light Horse Camp at Santa Cruz, which was my temporary home since taking up riding, approached my table. Beside him was a thickset man with greying hair, small eyes and an alert look.

"Hello, Bryant," said my acquaintance whose name was Arnold Harrison, and, turning to his companion, "Jim Shanks, Reg Bryant; mind if we sit down?"

"How d'you do," I said.

I had heard about Jim Shanks who was said to be a bit of a character, and knew that he had been away on home leave for six months. In fact he had only arrived back that morning on the Mail Boat, and was taking a breather from moving back into his flat in Colaba.

We ordered chota pegs and sampled the nuts on the table. While we chatted, Harrison kept looking across at me in a sidelong sort of way. I hadn't very much to say, naturally, nor did Shanks, who was unexpectedly silent about his recent furlough. Mainly he and Harrison spoke of the doings and whereabouts of their mutual acquaintances.

Shortly Shanks excused himself and left, crossing the lawn and out through the Clubhouse.

Harrison couldn't wait to talk about him, obviously, but first he said: "I hope you are coming to the Sausage Hunt on Sunday?"

I had heard talk of these events of which there were about three each Cold Weather. Usually at least twenty horsemen and women turned out. A suitable picnic spot, well beyond the outskirts of the City was selected, and riding there by any route, roundabout or otherwise, that they wished, the participants converged on it after meeting at a starting point some 8 or 10 miles nearer in. A day had to be chosen when the Bombay Hunt was not out as most of the interest came from those who hunted, many of whom were also members of the Bombay Light Horse, an auxiliary Cavalry Group ranked by civilians. An added attraction was the presence of several decorative females out for the season visiting relatives and who had managed to borrow a mount.

Non-riders, consisting of wives or friends, accompanied the riders in cars to the starting point, then went on to the chosen picnic spot. Here also, a lorry drew up containing a number of Bearers and a goodly supply of sausages, bacon, bread, eggs, beer and coffee. Syces, each with his master's horse, were waiting, having assembled them at day break from their various stables. Once everyone was off these syces would join the Bearers on the lorry and be ready to collect the horses at the destination.

The whole idea appealed immensely to me, and since there was nothing in the nature of a race about it I thought I could stay the course by now, having opted out of the last Sausage Hunt. "Yes, I'll be going," I said.

Harrison leaned over and spoke in a lower voice. "I couldn't mention this while Shanks was here," he said, "and I'll tell you why."

"Jim Shanks' family pretty well owns the Shipping Line whose Bombay agents he works for. He is well off and well connected. His actual surname is, or was, I am not sure which, Wathershanks, and his cousins have 'the Hon.' before their names, but he never shouted about it though it earns him tennis and other dates at Government House. He is an all-round sportsman and a fine rider who has dominated the Mud sports in the monsoon for many years. Fortyish, unmarried and a loner, he may have started off briefly in a Chummery, but I don't know where or when. He's lived alone for ages. He can afford to.

Many of the pretty and well-connected girls who come out for the Cold Weather are of the débutante type. They tend to make a beeline for Government House and its ADCs, and the more privileged Army circles who play polo for a pastime, but, of course, some 'Boxwallahs' with such a background as Jim Shanks also fall within their purview.

Thus it was that three years ago, almost to to-day, Shanks announced that his guest at the Sausage Hunt, on his second horse, would be the Lady Barbara Bowlton, a pretty young thing in her early twenties who had been making the pages in the 'Onlooker,' and an occasional Press society column.

Shanks was a sergeant in the Light Horse then, and a Hunt Whipper-in; map reading was his speciality. He told us when we all met that he would be taking Lady Barbara round a pretty and varied route by inlets of Vehar Lake where he'd told the adventurous girl that they might spot one or two crocodiles and other wildlife. It sounded exciting to some of the others, but they were tactful enough not to hint at going the same way. In fact, the destination, which is the same as arranged for us on Sunday, involved skirting both Lakes Powai and Vehar en route.

The horsemen took off in groups of various sizes, each with somebody who looked as if he knew where he was going to lead them. It was about 8.30 in the morning and warming up, so two hours riding, in and out of shade, would be about enough.

I was with George Simpson, his young sister out from home, Sandy McCabe and another girl, Agatha, daughter of a 'Burra Sahib' in Cotton, a tall pleasant girl who'd been out before somewhere up-country.

We followed the main paths, mostly, walking and trotting, and stopping for a breather or to look at the view. The countryside round the lakes consists of low hills, and some of the paths are contour-like. Higher up, it is all scrub jungle with a few larger and tangled trees and heavy exposed roots, partly covered by rotting vegetation which can be nasty snares and better kept away from. This, of course, would be well known to Shanks, however obscure his route, especially as Barbara's mount, a four-year-old black mare aptly named 'Cauchemar,' could be pretty nappy at times and capable of turning suddenly like the polo pony she occasionally was.

We expected that Shanks, in search of crocodiles, would wind around the lower reaches on the edge of Lake Vehar. Here the landscape is inhospitable and dishevelled, being thronged with innumerable toddy palms with palmetto-like fronds fanning out, some fallen and some at grotesque angles, the whole creating the effect of debris. One or two reed huts here and there, mostly abandoned, show a certain amount of human presence. Occasionally 'chokras' appear grinning and salaaming, asking for 'baksheesh' and fading away again.

Round about 10.30 the five of us homed in on the disused building, known as 'German Bungalow,' which formed the rendezvous, and dismounted. Some others were already there, and more kept appearing, all with a healthy appetite and thirst. The syces belonging to the early arrivals started to move off with their horses on the long walk back, eager for the siesta they would have earned.

No-one was surprised that Shanks and Lady Barbara were soon the only ones still absent.

"I think old Shanky is really taken by this young filly this time," remarked Sandy McCabe.

"A little more than a fatherly interest, eh?" added someone else, but beer and sausages were coming up and people converged on the knot of bearers who were starting to serve up the breakfast in earnest.

"From the broken down entrance gate to the compound of the building it was possible to see some two hundred yards down the track," Arnold Harrison went on, "and I was near this, holding a plate in one hand when the sound of galloping hooves first became audible. Those near to me looked up, and I was already staring down the lane when a horseman, none other than Jim Shanks, of course, came into view, and after covering about 100 yards, reined in and shouted, "Is Barbara there?"

"No," I yelled back, and without coming any nearer, Shanks wheeled round and made off at a gallop the way he had come.

"What on earth is he playing at?" asked George Simpson at my shoulder as we all looked at one another. "I'm going to see if I can get my horse," I said, "he's only been gone about ten minutes."

I found where my driver had parked the office car, got in and dashed off with him down the road taken by the syces, hoping that they had not struck across too long a stretch of countryside. In fact, I caught up with my syce and two others just before they left the road.

Telling the driver to bring the syce back to the rendezvous, I got on 'Warrior,' trotted back to the gathering, grabbed a roll and a couple of sausages and set off in search of Shanks and Lady Barbara. Of course, I was puzzled as we all were, but in Shanks' voice there had been the sort of tone he put in on parade when things weren't to his liking. More so, in fact, on this occasion.

As I trotted along I wondered what it meant. Had the two had a row and Barbara gone ahead on her own, though not really knowing the way? This would account for Shanks' extraordinary question as to whether she had arrived at the rendezvous. Yet somehow, I didn't think it was that. I had a nasty sort of sinking feeling that worse had occurred.

At that point, I cut into Arnold Harrison's narrative and ordered a couple more 'chota pegs.' "Jim Shanks being the sort of outdoor man he evidently is, and looks, how could he possibly lose the only person he was riding with?" I asked.

"Exactly," replied Arnold, "that's just what was bothering me. Anyhow," he went on, "I could only carry on down the track on the lookout for some sort of clue or sign or sound, couldn't I?"

A mile on the track divided, one arm sloping downwards and the other, which was the one we ourselves had followed, continuing on the same level.

So I went downwards. It grew pretty tangled, and twice I had to get off and lead 'Warrior' over nasty uneven ground through the nullah, and here I saw fresh hoofmarks. Suddenly 'Warrior' whinnied, and in a hollow, her reins caught round a large fallen branch, was the the black mare 'Cauchemar.' There were scratches round her head and neck, and a gash on her left knee, making her, as I saw on freeing her, very lame. Otherwise, her equipment was all in place.

I brought her up, tethered her on the track in the shade, doing what I could for her knee, and carried on down towards the toddy palms ringing the lake. As the ground cleared I could see Shanks' other horse standing still, but no sign of Shanks himself. "Jim," I shouted, "are you there?" Silence.

I went on down slowly and reached the other horse, then dismounted and stood very still. I thought I had heard something. Then it came again, like a low moan of pain, and only about ten yards away I saw a kneeling figure in a clump of coarse bush and reeds. It was Shanks, with his head in his hands, and he was sweating and shaking as if he had malaria.

"Good God, Jim," I blurted out, putting my hand on his shoulder, "what's happened, where's Barbara? Didn't you see her horse up there?"

Shanks shuddered, made as if to rise and slumped down again. He turned and seemed to put a glassy stare through and past me, then: "Aagh, God, what an impossible thing," he shouted out. Then slowly he focussed on me. "Arnold Harrison, naturally someone had to follow me and make it real. Of course I've seen 'Cauchemar' now, you fool. She must have been trying to get up to the road ever since I lost them."

"Lost them?" I essayed.

"Barbara's over there, not far above here. She's dead! Is anyone else with you?" I couldn't say anything, so he repeated his question more urgently.

"All the syces have gone back by now. I'm alone," I

replied. "I just managed to chase up mine and get hold of 'Warrior.'

This news seemed to restore Shanks to some sanity, but I stayed where I was and waited a good two minutes before he finally said, pointing, "You'd better go and look."

Lady Barbara Bowlton was indeed dead. She had not worn a topee, but a double terai, headgear rather favoured by the younger ladies, consisting of a wide brimmed, usually green, felt hat lined by a smaller white one, normally fairly safe for hacking in the open, but perhaps not for Shanks' Sausage Hunt routes.

It was pretty clear to me what had happened and that the soft hat was very likely responsible for her death. There was a large ugly bruise across her forehead and the skin was lacerated. Her position was contorted, and I braced myself to move her and confirm that her neck was broken. The awful thing was that her body was still warm. She may have tried to hail Shanks as he galloped along the road 200 yards higher up.

I guessed that 'Cauchemar' must have bolted, and this, among trees, commonly results in a bad fall if a branch sweeps a rider to the ground. Wearing that terai, Barbara wouldn't see a branch coming head high and be able to duck in time. A topee tends to slip on to the back of the head and one can see under the brim. Full of dread, I returned to Jim Shanks.

He appeared to have recovered some of his usual phlegm. "You saw?" he said. "She's broken her neck?"

"Yes, I'm afraid so. How truly awful. One of us will have to go back and break the news, but first, do you want to tell me what happened?"

"Arnold, you've got to believe me when I say I lost

them. We were on ahead half a mile over there and I was going to go up the last path leading up from the lake and come out on the other side of the Bungalow, which I've done before. We were trotting along the track by the reeds when round a corner we came on a large crocodile actually half-way across. Instead of going on it stopped, and then whirled round and back into the lake. This brought us very near to it, and both horses panicked. While I was trying to calm 'Jason,' 'Cauchemar' reared up, turned about and bolted off the way we had come, and I had no chance to see anything more except that Barbara was holding her seat well.

"Normally a horse would dash up the wider track you first came down and on to the straight bit leading to our destination. I thought I'd try that first, but now it's clear that 'Cauchemar' turned off earlier, probably because Barbara was trying to pull her in while she was still frightened."

"It wasn't your fault," I said.

"But it was really, I'm responsible, aren't I?"

"Well, yes," I admitted, "but . . ."

"You know my reputation," cut in Shanks, his voice rising again. "Adventuring, and doing unusual things, but doing them well always, and successfully. How will I ever live this down?"

It was then that the man's character became clearer to me. He was actually more concerned about his own ego than poor Lady Barbara, and the other effects of her fatal accident which now began to assail me.

"I won't go into detail about what followed and how the news was taken at the breakfast. Nor how we brought back Lady Barbara and the horses, helped by other horrified sausage hunters, and Shanks' and my syces,"

Harrison continued.

Those servants who were still at the picnic site seemed incredulous, and huddled round together exchanging theories, but soon, used to death and disaster in their own existences, they rallied round eager to help.

When everyone had mustered and the lorry had gone off ahead, the cars moved off, forming, all too realistically, a funeral cortege.

Up to then it had been left to me, to my distaste, to tell what I knew, because Shanks, busying himself with his two horses, remained aloof and completely incommunicado, never hardly raising his eyes from the ground. Had he been wearing his sergeant's stripes I had a picture of him tearing them off his arm in a gesture of complete resignation.

I merely said: "The horses evidently bolted different ways, and they lost each other." I didn't mention the crocodile, because I realised that I would have to be at the inquest which was bound to come. Many people might scoff at the thought of a crocodile across the pathway, but sportsmen know that these creatures will travel a long way by land from one stretch of water to another, though usually by night.

There was, of course, a terrible outcry, not improved by Shank's total refusal to be interviewed by the Press. This meant that reporters from 'The Times of India,' and, more insistently, 'The Bombay Chronicle,' though not excluding the Light Horse Camp, pretty well haunted me at the office for the next few days.

Soon on the warpath for anybody and everybody involved were Lady Barbara's father, the Earl of Crostan, the Countess, the son and heir and a prominent British lawyer, who all arrived in Bombay for the inquest which, as it happened, was conducted in impeccable style.

The finger of opprobrium was levelled very pointedly at Shanks, and my own evidence, being largely the account of the circumstances related to me by Shanks himself, was a bit thin, but I had been able to trace most of the path taken by the horse 'Cauchemar' below and above where Barbara had fallen, and could swear that no other rider had been there. I convinced the Coroner that I had enough woodcraft for that. Also the cause of death was irrefutable.

Shanks, in court, was a pathetic sight, making no attempt to smarten himself up, and not improving matters by taking an aggressive stand towards questions put to him. I knew why this was, of course. He was still treating the whole thing as a slight, implying callous neglect on his part, with no thought in his head of any more direct implication in Lady Barbara's actual death, at which at least one newspaper had been hinting.

In fact, it was this very attitude that tended to take suspicion away from him and satisfy the Coroner that the whole thing was an accident, and that being off-sighted round a corner, Shanks was in no position to remedy things. If Shanks thought he, with his years of reputed jungle lore, could have done so, it didn't actually matter to the Coroner. As to the crocodile, more than a few people in the Court had seen the notices round Vehar Lake saying 'Beware of Crocodiles.'

Finally, the Coroner's verdict of accidental death was generally acceptable, even by Lady Barbara's bereaved family, the legal books were closed, and Shanks cleared of blame, it being the Coroner's opinion, summing up, that the facts were clear. The incident, he said, had occurred close to the end of the ride, and even if Shanks was hasty in taking the action he did, it actually proved that he neither witnessed the fatal event, nor had the time or need to fabricate it.

Dusk was spreading over the Yacht Club lawn, lights were going on, and boating members of the Club were mooring their yachts and coming up the steps.

Arnold Harrison stretched. "I tell you, Reg, I was glad it was all over, but Jim Shanks will never be the same again. He no longer competes or socialises, beyond token appearances at a Club, like this evening when it was special. If you could call it that, I have become, perhaps his best friend, but I have the feeling that he is going to leave India soon.

"If the War that looks like coming happens, that could be his salvation. He'll be a damn' good soldier."

# THE OLD KOI HAI

It is best, when about to go out to India, to have a completely open mind, because however many stories are told about it, the reality compared to life anywhere else is well-nigh impossible to capture in advance. Facts and figures, of course, are helpful, but although enough books have been written about true and imaginary situations, no tourism had reached India by the time Denis Fairbairn went out there.

The people who might best have given Denis a foretaste of what to expect, at the same time answering his unspoken questions, were his contemporaries who had recently gone before him. However, as few newly-posted men returned home before four years, such friends were still there.

So he contented himself with what he could find out in his Company's head office in London, and made notes of his own of what salient points of information seemed to be necessary for him in any event.

He was given an outfit allowance of £50 for metal trunks and tropical weight clothes and here, some people were helpful, though not particularly so a shop in Piccadilly reputed to specialise in such things.

They suggested a topee with a neck protection Foreign Legion style, a mosquito net, spine pads and everything else in Sea Island cotton as well as two natty suits.

It would have made short work of double Denis's allowance.

Fortunately, a man home on leave from Burma turned up at the office and told him, simply, that he could get all the proper things he needed, other than for the voyage out, as soon as he got to Bombay, but that he should take a couple of zinc-lined black tin trunks.

All the same, after buying the correct 'Bombay Bowler' topee at Simon Arzt's in Port Said, and entering the Suez Canal, Fairbairn trotted out for dinner the white cotton drill monkey jacket he had fallen for in London. This, except for his black cummerbund, unfortunately turned out to be matched by the dining room stewards, and he quickly reverted to his normal dinner jacket.

Not many weeks after getting off the P & O boat in Bombay, Fairbairn knew just where he stood sartorially, even down to washable white cloth wrist watch straps.

He was given to understand soon after his arrival that he was a 'Chokrah.' A chokrah, in fact, was any Indian boy from about seven to twenty years old, and for a European it loosely signified that he was the junior assistant in his office. Fairbairn was never sure if the sobriquet attached for the whole of a first contract, or just for about a year, like a first-termer at school.

After that there seemed to be no intermediate title until one became the boss and automatically a 'Burra Sahib' with a Burra Memsahib if he had a wife.

As the age of 50 or even 55 drew near, if not before, members of the business community and certain Services became known as 'Old Koi Hais.' There was no such thing, apparently, as a young Koi Hai.

Now the rough meaning of koi hai in English is 'anyone there?' It is, in fact, called out at the same time as a white sahib, or other master, claps his hands to summon a servant for service of some kind, either at home or in the Club.

The connection was never explained to Denis Fairbairn during his stay in India, so he could only assume that old koi hais had spent years shouting it out in this way.

It was a title given out of affection for the holder as much as anything else.

So to be an old koi hai, it was not necessary to be a burra sahib. It was more a question of age or having been in India, with furloughs in between, for upwards of twenty five years. Koi hais did not long for or accept transfers back to Britain. They worked out their years in India thereby confirming their status. Some of them stayed on even after Independence, or are to be found to this day in Surrey, Sussex or Hampshire.

Denis found that opportunities for sport were many, mostly through membership of the local Gymkhana Club which could be joined in a matter of days, granted suitability. Unsuitable were Europeans in the retail shopkeeping trade whose social centre was the Commercial Gymkhana where they rubbed shoulders with people in the minor Civil services such as the Post Office and local Government, and where they even played Bowls. Non-expatriates were members also.

Later, there were more exclusive Clubs and Golf Clubs or Riding Clubs to join, as one chose.

Most old koi hais, having gone through the gamut of the more fast-moving competitive sports, confined themselves to tennis at the Gymkhana, but not a few hunted, or sailed, or played golf at the Willingdon Club.

Of course, Denis Fairbairn did not learn these things in a very short time. Chokrahs were expected to ask questions to begin with, naturally, but over-eagerness to delve into the accepted social attitudes and behaviour patterns had people edging away. The established order of life for British residents culminated in Government House, and though some, like Denis Fairbairn, did not care particularly, other young single men behaved as if they were constantly under surveillance about doing the right thing.

It took about a year before Denis became really friendly with an old koi hai who, like himself, was a keen tennis player. His name was Arthur Lane, and he was the General Manager of the Bombay, Baroda and Central India Railway, the B.B. & C.I.

He had come out to India in 1917 on secondment from the Royal Engineers to the Royal Bombay Sappers and Miners, and was snapped up by the Railways as soon as the War ended. He was then 27.

Arthur Lane, C.I.E., the old koi hai, had never married.

He had a fine B.B. & C.I. bungalow on Malabar Hill and was neither short of company nor servants. Bachelors of his age were rare. Although at 46 he had less than five years to retirement he had no more than a slight paunch, kept as fit as the climate would allow, had a good skin, dark hair with just a suspicion of grey, and a strong 180 lb, 5 feet ll inch frame.

Denis Fairbairn admired him. He was an all-round attractive man, and had he spent his Hot Weathers in hill stations, the memsahibs, temporarily exiled there, would have given him little peace.

It was he who told Denis all he wanted to know about society trends and significant events in Bombay's short Cold Weather season.

"Perhaps that is the only time when people drop their obsession with the awful hot humid weather and the steamy discomfort of the three-month-long monsoon, counting on their fingers how long it could be before they got on the mailboat home," Arthur said.

"I was luckier, because, after a six-month course of grooming here in Bombay, the B.B. & CI. sent me up-

country on field work, you could call it. I was stationed at
Ajmer for several years and then at Surat, then in and
out of that lovely place, Udaipur. Apart from Surat, the
climate was dry and the Cold Weather lasted for four
and a half months on average."

As time went by, Denis Fairbairn, in the cotton
business, needed to visit mills and ginning factories in
Gujarat and Kathiawar, and Lane's years up-country
provided him with useful advice. It was not unlikely
that Arthur Lane should not have married. It was no
life, as Denis saw, for a woman then, except perhaps for a
very special one, and she had not come along evidently.

As it was, the sensitive and romantic streaks that
Arthur had, thrived in an environment free from the
noise and feverish tempo of the City. It would be wrong
to say that large Indian cities were not India; they could
be nowhere else. But the changeless India, the mystical,
ancient, wise, beautiful, and harsh India, lies in the
uncrowded inland jungles, plains, forests and hills.

Many Europeans have spent years of their lives in the
Country and left it remembering only as if they saw it all
through a window, unless, of course, their duties led
them away far inland.

When he was in Ajmer Arthur Lane was struck by the
change in the people and their garb, the women
particularly. Instead of the rather squat Mahratta types of
Bombay with their ugly dhoti style tucked in sarees,
around him now were stately Rajput beauties, many
nearly as tall as he. Over flimsy trousers, their multi-
coloured long skirts came almost down to the ground
and swirled as they moved.

As they bore brass pots, or merchandise, on their heads,
they did not waddle to keep them horizontally in place,

but glided, walking straight from the hip.

Arthur wondered about these women who did not display the evident signs of self-effacing submissiveness of their simple sisters further south. Troupes of strolling players, musicians and dancers, came into Ajmer from time to time, and the self-assured female performers were highly attractive with their graceful carriage, their features heightened by make-up and tight 'Bowlee' bodices, their ankles adorned with thick and heavy bangles and tinkling nursery bells.

"These are bad people," Arthur's Indian assistants told him; while the Anglo-Indian officials simply said: "Prostitutes."

The idea intrigued Arthur who had only seen those who gesticulated from their 'cages' in Grant Road in Bombay. He was not anxious to try his manhood out on them, but knew that he would be attracted if some kind of safe system operated with such delectable wares.

One day he asked one of his Indian colleagues, a line Inspector called Mhaisalkar, what passed for night life in Ajmer.

"You want to see a dancer, Lane sahib?" Mhaisalkar suggested. He wrote a note with a street address on it.

"Go there at about ten 10 o'clock tonight," he said.

Arthur found the house easily, among a row of others in a street just off the main bazaar of the native town. He went up the stone staircase where he heard music and into a bare square room dimly lit by a large oil lamp in a window niche. A shielded overhead electric bulb and a few candles in other niches completed the lighting.

Six or seven men sat cross-legged on the floor in a circle, complemented by three musicians with 'Tablas,' a 'Sarangi,' and a 'Sitar.' Lane stopped at the entrance, because the dancer within the circle was twirling towards the close of her number.

As she finished, the shadowy figures of the men watching stirred and cast odd rupee coins at her feet. She picked these up and glided out by a doorway behind the musicians who did not seem to be included in this largesse.

Heads hardly turned as Lane found a place and sat on the floor among the circle. The smell of incense, or something like it, was strong. The music started up again, and the same dancer reappeared. She was of indeterminate age, small and skinny rather than slender, but her command of the dance was fluid and professional, illustrating the story with the posture of her hands and fingers.

When this dance ended Lane threw in a couple of rupees, and ten minutes later, there was another dance followed by a ripple of movement in the audience who, salaaming, and with a final contribution, got up, drifted down the stairs, and melted into the night, Lane following.

Clearly, no exciting sequences nor veiled eyes in scented gardens with tinkling fountains were to be a part of the night life of Ajmer, nor any other small provincial town.

Mhaisalkar was contrite about this; "Lane sahib," he said, "you would have to be a guest in the palace of a Rajput prince on a rare occasion of feasting, to see, do you call it? an orgy, and receive the favours of a dancing girl, even if the British Resident was one such sahib who would close an eye to such a thing."

People whose jobs involved spending their days in the heart of India, as did Arthur Lane, had much to delight the senses and even quiet the inevitable urges of the body. Stories went round that these urges were sometimes quelled by experiences on shikar, the hunting with rifle and shot-gun of the animals and birds of the jungle. Strange things, it was told, happened when a hunter caught up with a freshly killed wild peacock or a dying beast.

The spell Lane had had in Surat mercifully extended to no more than six months. It was the end of a line, literally, and required no more than the money needed for its reasonable maintenance. He could sense for a while the atmosphere of the British East India Company and tried to imagine the details of its establishment when he went and picked his way through the old gateway at the original Tapti landing where the river joined the sea at the now dilapidated Port.

The town of Surat was squalid and had only one hotel. It could no longer pretend to have any social life to offer Europeans, but there were some good Indian families of the merchant class of Marwaris who, despite their bad name for greed and the obsession with money, entertained readily and lavishly.

One of these, Mr Lalchand Joshi, was sorry to see Lane go.

"Why do you not get the B.B. & C.I. to run three, instead of two, trains a week, Sahib," he said. "You have seen, surely, that Surat is an important stop for Country craft?"

This was a fact. Dhows called from as far away as the Persian Gulf and Mombasa, and smaller craft covered the small ports from Baluchistan down the Malabar coast to Cochin, as well as Karachi and Bombay, returning with spices, sandalwood, country tiles, salted fish, coir matting and much else.

Lane, strolling on the almost untrodden palm-fringed beaches in the comparative cool of the early morning, had thrilled to the sight of the dhows, the rising sunlight on their triangular sails, the smallest ones with dawn fishermen and the large ones making for or leaving the Port.

These were the boats that Joshi and his like had much concern for. There were big profits to be made financing these voyages, buying and selling the goods, and haggling over the freight cost with distant owners other than they themselves. No wonder the Marwaris would welcome more railway trucks.

Before leaving, Lane said he would do what he could. It would certainly form part of his report as soon as he could get it back to Ainsley, his Divisional manager at Ajmer.

Leslie Ainsley was a decent enough man. He had been in up-country centres almost all his service with the B.B. & C.I. and now was due for retirement in four or five years at 55.

He had, perhaps, made the mistake of getting on too well with the Anglo-Indians who formed the core of Railway staff. The Railway Institute was their Club to which Europeans, but not Indians, were freely welcomed. It was impossible for a senior official like Ainsley not to attend Institute functions and dances, but in Bombay it was thought that he had overdone it.

Mrs Ainsley, when she was not visiting the children in England, went along with what her husband did, but as far as Arthur was concerned she was a good reason why he did not want to be left too long in Ajmer.

Dora Ainsley was in her early forties, tall, statuesque,

dark and with good features, but expressionless, the kind of person you could never tell what she was thinking, and only in time could you guess if she was intelligent, shy or completely vapid.

She had no sex-appeal and never seemed to say very much, giving the impression that she abhorred small talk; an unusual thing in a woman expatriate, and another reason, perhaps, why Ainsley had not evidently hankered after the social life of a burra sahib in Bombay.

Arthur Lane, who was interested in the people he came across, had no inhibitions and liked to be open, soon took a dislike to Dora Ainsley who gave out so few clues to her personality. It was irritating to any third party that when she and her husband thought they were alone, there was a constant buzz of conversation, the source of which it was hard to imagine.

One thing seemed to be obvious and that was that Leslie Ainsley and his wife were devoted to one another, and Dora left nothing to be desired in the way she managed their home, using the servants about the bungalow as little as she respectably could.

In spite of himself, Arthur could not help the fact that Dora made him feel uneasy, and as he had to spend the greater part of each day with either or both of the Ainsleys he found things getting more and more on his nerves.

He was tempted to try and draw Dora out, but got nowhere, even after she had been in England for two months.

"How did you find the children this time, Dora?" he asked her brightly.

"Oh, all right," she said. "They are growing up, of course."

"You must miss them a lot in these in-between years."

"Naturally."

Even this subject did not get Mrs Ainsley going, and Arthur dropped any idea of asking the obvious following questions about what the kids were good at, and gave up. Normally easy going and friendly, Arthur admired femininity and feared he might lose patience with Dora Ainsley and cause disruption.

So when, one day, Leslie hesitantly approached him and said: "Arthur, old boy, we really need someone now to go over and supervise the end of the new line to Udaipur," Arthur brightened up.

"It means you'd be virtually camping out in the jungle," Leslie went on apologetically, "but it would be good experience for you."

Arthur affected an attitude of condescending dutifulness.

"Of course I'll go," he said.

Leslie looked relieved. "Right, I'll tell Head Office in Bombay, and get Percy Roberts to come here and brief you."

Percy Roberts, an Anglo-Indian, was the man in charge of the work force on the Udaipur line and, like most of his colleagues, so far from resenting a European overseer, saw the close relationship with someone like Lane as more of a feather in his cap.

"Yes, Mr Lane," he said. "We will make you as comfortable as we can. There is a good little used forest inspection bungalow near enough to Udaipur that we can commandeer and fit out for you and your wife."

"I am not married," said Arthur.

"Never mind, we can get one of the beauties of Pichola Lake to come and 'do' for you." Roberts stopped wondering then if he had gone too far in familiarity, catching a look from Leslie Ainsley.

Arthur smiled indulgently, his curiosity nonetheless aroused.

The next few days were taken up getting together his own things as well as domestic items that Roberts claimed were necessary, plus a few perks for himself.

Udaipur State is entered through a long valley guarded at the end by a narrow pass bounded on both sides by precipitous rock cliffs. Down this valley the railway was being constructed to join with the Baroda/Ajmer section of the main line. In that setting, the coming months were to provide Arthur Lane with the happiest time of his life in India, and the most significant.

The Maharana of Udaipur, an orthodox and thrifty ruler, seldom emerged from his palace/fortress. He was entirely conscious of his inheritance as the senior prince of all the Rajput Native States, a legacy held secure through the years by the impregnable position of his territory; nor was he in favour of the proposed free access to it by means of the railway. Even less so when requested by the Government of India Political Department to provide some of the funds for its construction from his own coffers.

Roberts was unaware of this and just carried out orders from above. The Viceroy himself, apprised of the Maharana's objections, had made the necessary personal amends. Work was thus continuing unhampered.

In a way it seemed to Arthur Lane a unique assignment, both timely and intriguing.

Lake Pichola, the predominant feature of Udaipur, was a thing of shimmering natural beauty surrounded by parched hills, which exploded into greenery round its borders. It reminded Lane of Lake Maggiore in Italy, and in place of Isola Bella was the Maharana's island summer palace. Only the lawns with flowers and fountains and strutting white peafowl were open to the simply curious, the buildings beyond, polished jewels of white marble, to the privileged few.

Facing this across the water and on the lake-shore border of the town, stood the vast, and equally mysterious, main palace, a conglomerate of gleaming towers and cupolas, courtyards, high walls and ramparts, a citadel indeed as well as a luxurious domain.

In an area as wide as two tennis courts a six foot wall stood where the net would be. Long rows of steps along a high terrace on the town side accommodated ordinary spectators. This yard was still the stage for elephant fights, watched from on high by the Maharana and his entourage.

A little way out of the town, nestling within its walls, and along a dusty track, built tower-like into the rocky side of a steep cliff was a wide round pit with an access door at the bottom and a broken down viewing platform at the top. This was once the scene of another popular entertainment; fights between a tiger and a wild boar or a lion from the Gir Forest. This sport, however, Percy Roberts said, was banned about the beginning of the century.

Roberts showed Lane all these things on their first shopping expedition in the Company's car. There did not seem to be much else happening, but the breath taking setting was enough in itself to delight and awake Arthur's imagination. I am going to be in my element here, he thought.

All the gear that he decided he needed was soon

installed in the Inspection bungalow. This was in typical style and not very large. Rectangular in shape, it had a central room entered up the verandah steps and through a heavy door wedged open. In the middle of the room was a large table with four chairs around it, and on the near side by one of the two front windows an easy chair of sorts and another one with arms.

On either side of the room an opening led to a smaller sized bedroom, and through at the back to a washroom with a tin bath, a 'Chilumchi,' or basin, and a thunderbox. This one also had a wooden towel rail, a clothes line, and even a crude, curtainless, shower.

Around the sides of the bungalow ran the verandah, enclosed by a metre-high open-work solid wood railing below which a few flowers nodded stalwartly. A couple of teak siesta chairs with a long scooped cane back lounging surface and a leg rest on each side were placed near the front entrance.

Arthur Lane liked it, and the glade almost cut out of the jungle which faced it. A rough drive ran round to the back of the bungalow and on to the road, a quarter mile below which was the railway track.

Also, some fifty yards to the rear, were the khansama's quarters and a couple of rooms for other servants. Lane's bearer, Lalji, he had allowed to go and visit his family near Surat.

The khansama, Motiram, a little wiry man, seemed to do everything; cooking, gardening and housekeeping, all unobtrusively.

Percy Roberts lived in a newly built white-washed brick house down by the line, with his wife, Edna. Percy was pot-bellied, cheerful and continuing friendly, and Edna was fat and jolly and anxious for Lane's welfare. Like many of her community, she cooked extremely well, and knew about the wild fruits and herbs of the jungle, besides using what game the gun would bring in.

The khansama's specialities ranged little further than 'Murgee,' or chicken, omelettes, soup from beans and pulses, and scraggy pieces of pork, followed by caramel custard known traditionally as 'Dak bungalow pudding.'

The completed railway line and following rolling stock were drawing nearer. At each stage for two or three miles gangs were at work on whatever was required to progress to the next point in a sort of leap frog operation.

Arthur spent his days coordinating these stages, sometimes with Percy Roberts and sometimes on his own. In the evening as long as it was light he explored the jungle in the vicinity of the bungalow. May had come around and it was extremely hot and dry.

Lane had done some riding in the early morning on one of two horses that Percy Roberts had acquired, along with a syce, from somewhere in the town, and he wondered how it would be if he tried going through the jungle on it up to the foothills beyond.

He put it to Roberts on one of the three or four evenings each week he had a meal with him and Edna, thankful for the diversion as well as getting away from Motiram's monotonous fare.

"What do you think of that idea?" he asked Percy.

"It's not a pastime I have heard much about, nor would I do it myself," said Percy, "but at this time of the year it should be pretty easy going if you start early and don't go too far. You ought to see quite a lot though the animals will always see you first. There is very little shikar around here so they are fairly tame, but they won't hang around."

"But what about on horseback?" asked Arthur.

"Quite different. Four legs are to be expected. Two legs the wild animals never really trust. Anyhow try it," Percy said. "I'll send the syce up with the older horse at dawn tomorrow, but be careful of protruding branches and large stones. There are no tigers in this area, so the only beast you must be wary of is the sloth bear. Short sighted, lazy and maybe drunk on mowa berries, you could stumble on him and get thrown. Don't get lost by the way!"

After that, thankful for the way Roberts had taken it, Arthur looked forward eagerly to each morning he could arrange.

The feeling he had, mounted on the patient and steady horse, Kumar, was to have become a part of the wild things in their own realm. The smaller deer, ever active, never showed themselves for long. Cheetal, the beautiful spotted deer, standing as if in shafts of sunlight through dappling leaves, clustered where there were nullahs not yet quite dry, and grass and weeds still lined the banks. Feeling fairly secure in their numbers, their heads quickly went up on the approach of Kumar.

Lane learned to hold off when he was near enough to any animal to get a good view. The moment he spurred Kumar towards them they scented a chase; particularly the majestic, but shy, Sambar, not for a moment taking Kumar for one of themselves.

The fecund wild pig abounded in sounders of varying numbers, and those Kumar did not like, the careless little squeakers once or twice almost getting under his feet. Mowa trees were many, and the scent of their fleshy, jelly-like little flowers fermenting on the ground, was powerful. Only one bear did Arthur see, fast asleep in his own paradise.

Coming out of the jungle edge on to a dried up area of paddy fields one morning Lane flushed out three Nilgai, two blue bulls, and one beige/brown cow. He decided to try and get close to these strange looking antelope and urged Kumar into a gallop across the first field. The Nilgai then broke into a languid, but sustained, canter, keeping up the same pace over flat and bund, and Arthur was surprised to find that he could not ride Kumar even to within sixty or seventy yards of them.

He reined in, re-established his bearings, and found his way back to the bungalow.

"Don't forget when we next go in to Udaipur to remind me to show you the bathing beauties of Gangor Ghat." Percy said, at their dinner that evening, at the same time giving Arthur an exaggerated wink for Edna's benefit.

Until Percy gave the promised demonstration Arthur happily carried on filling each day until he dropped into bed ready for a good sleep.

Beside the outer wall of the Maharana's winter palace was the bathing ghat, the steps down forming a wedge in the wall's angle so that there was only one way in and out.

Percy Roberts led Arthur as near as possible outside the span of the wall obviously pleased with himself as a guide. From fifteen to twenty women of varying ages were using the ghat. Percy saw Arthur's wide-eyed look.

"What do you think about that, Arthur?" It was hardly a question.

Arthur did not reply at once. The women were bathing and sluicing themselves with the water of the lake with a lot of attention to their hair. Sodden garments clung transparently to most of them, but half a dozen young girls were naked to the waist, splashing and ducking up and down.

Arthur was talking to himself more than answering Percy's question.

"Beautiful," he said.

He became aware of how he had felt following the movements and sway of their bodies when watching the younger women of Rajputana going their ways in Ajmer, but to see these half-naked girls gaily laughing together, the water glistening on their smooth brown skins and taughtening their rounded breasts, stirred the urges in him that he had sought to sublimate on his jungle forays with Kumar.

The girls knew that they were being watched by the two European men, but unlike the older ones who shrank away and covered themselves with the wet ends of their sarees, they simpered and giggled together.

Arthur and Percy turned away then, Arthur with a mixed feeling of reluctance and relief; the unadorned appeal of the Rajput maidens had done more to his sensibilities than he cared to admit.

Percy, who had a nubile enough wife, looked satisfied. Besides, conscious of his own blood, he would not touch an Indian. He smirked at Arthur.

"Brazen little hussies, some of them, weren't they?"

Arthur looked at him rather sharply. Whatever man-talk Percy wanted to use, it was not a description that came to him, he thought. Magical would have expressed it better, but he managed a pleasant reply.

"Many thanks, Percy," he said. "I was wondering what you meant when you talked about the beauties of Lake Pichola back in Ajmer. I bet they don't do that in Benares."

"I won't take you up on that," Percy said. "Do you mind if I collect a few things for the memsahib? Then we'll get back."

Chatting together one day after one of Edna's meals, Percy asked Arthur where his bearer was.

"Still near Surat at his village as far as I know," Arthur told him.

"The way things are going," Percy said, "how long do you think it might be before you can get away from here?"

Lane considered. "Would you say in two or three months?" he asked, "I was hinting at that in my last report to Mr Ainsley at Ajmer."

"Yes, we should be ready for the finishing touches to the line by then. After that its routine."

"What I mean is," Percy went on, getting to the point, "there is a woman who did some housekeeping for us further back down the line who wants to get her eldest daughter into something like that in order to improve her chances of making a good marriage. You've got the khansama, Motiram, and your bearer may not relish it here nor get on with my moslem chap, old Jeetakhan."

"My bearer thinks I am still in Ajmer, I imagine," Lane said. "I can get word to him to stay on in his 'mullokh'. He'd be delighted."

A few days later, suitably on a Sunday, Percy drove up in the Company car.

"She's the mother," he said, jerking a thumb at the handsome woman who had alighted. "Name of Nanabhai."

The woman, probably still in her thirties, but middle aged in demeanour, salaamed, inclining from the waist hands together, fingers pointing at Lane. "Salaam

Nanabhai," he responded.

"She's come to look you and the bungalow over," Roberts explained. "Says she knows of Motiram, and is 'his cousin sister'."

The deferential Nanabhai made little more than a cursory inspection, and said she would come back tomorrow bringing her daughter, Shanti. The quarters at the back, near Motiram's, evidently were adequate.

Arthur Lane was not really prepared for Shanti. Probably about 17 years old, the delicacy of her whole bearing, her coffee-coloured flawless skin and small, well-chiselled features made her seem like an old print of a Mogul princess.

She and Nanabhai arrived in a tonga. Lane unobtrusively watched them unpacking bedding rolls, bundles of what looked like clothing, a few pots, some foodstuffs, and a sort of oversized basketwork hamper, Motiram helping them.

Motiram, in no way resentful, now confined himself to the kitchen, the garden and the collecting of food. The latter came from sources unknown to Lane who, when he was not at home making notes and calculations, spent his working days down on the site of the railway line. This had now gone well beyond the nearby settlement where Roberts and his workers were, but there was no need to move this any nearer to Udaipur.

The evening of the new arrivals was one of those that Lane had set aside for writing up his reports on the big table in the centre room, after Motiram's meal had come and gone. He thought he had detected a new flavour in the chicken and wondered if Nanabhai had had anything to do with it.

A few drops of premature monsoon rain had fallen

briefly and it was a bit fresher. He moved the paraffin storm lantern closer and found, for once, that his forearms were not sticking to the paper. He became absorbed in what he wrote, his thoughts flowing freely. When he finished he wondered if his explorations on Kumar would soon have to be over, and went outside. The rain was gone, leaving no obvious trace.

Absorbed, he had not noticed a soundless shadow move behind his back into his bedroom. Shanti. The little oil lamp at his bedside was ready with matches; the mosquito net straightened. A shaft of moonlight came through the barred window. He took up the lamp into the bathroom and went back to the bedroom, sliding under the net, too tired to pick up his Hindi book.

During the week Lane noticed a good many changes for his comfort. It was as if Lalji had come back without being always a bit in the way. Motiram's menus also got steadily better.

Nanabhai, Shanti behind her, appeared on the verandah one morning as Lane handed Kumar over to the syce after his ride.

"Lane sahib," she said, in effect, "I am going back to Udaipur to look after my younger children. Shanti will now stay and keep house for you. She has been shown all what to do. If you are dissatisfied, send a message by one of Roberts sahib's workers or Motiram. Salaam sahib."

Shanti moved to the side, sloe eyes a bit downcast, but the suspicion of an ingratiating smile showed at the corners of her full lips. Arthur Lane felt his mouth go dry.

He turned and hurried into the bungalow to collect a few rupees. He heard a tonga coming up the track.

Motiram got out of it and went round to get Arthur's bath while Arthur handed Nanabhai the money, accepted her salaams, and went in to change.

Thoughts about Shanti came into Arthur's mind during the day. He wondered if indeed she had ever been among the girls at Gangor Ghat. Taller than her mother, five feet five inches at a guess, and fairer, no garments could hide the soft and full symmetrical lines of her body and slender limbs. The maidens at the ghat only spoke half of what Shanti might conceal, he thought.

Arthur found himself looking forward to the end of the day's work and getting home to the bungalow as never before. He avoided Percy Roberts like the plague, wondering if he knew what had taken place.

Shanti had finished for the day when Arthur got back. Motiram looked pleased with himself. Obviously he had now less to do. The meal was good.

Afterwards, as Arthur, having made liberal use of the Flit gun, lounged on the verandah with his legs up and a drink in the glass-holder of the chair, he thought hard about Shanti. He expected she had learned dancing like most little Indian girls. Her hands, with long slim fingers, seemed made to tell a story of the Ramayana. He would love to touch, and be touched by her.

Of course, by now, with the War two years past and gone, even British Army other ranks got home on furlough occasionally, and the shame of consorting with Indian women pervaded European society at all levels. Regular passenger steamers had eased the burden of tedious years.

Hindu morals, too, had to be reckoned with more. Whatever had inevitably happened in the past involving soldiers going native and retiring in the district of Bangalore, the result had been to create a sizeable Anglo-Indian community there for them to join if they wished.

Just as Hindus respected a religious man of any faith so they approved of one who held their womenfolk as inviolate as a memsahib or a missie-sahib was to them, strange though their doings within their own community might seem.

Arthur Lane couldn't help it. For more reasons than one he was ready to fall in love with Shanti, and this presented him with a problem in his yearning. A pity, he thought, that this was not like the South Seas where Polynesian sirens were reputed to have neither inhibitions of their own nor were in any way averse to sharing their charms with the European male.

If a third party had looked at Shanti closely, he, or she more likely, would notice signs of devotion to Lane that were not only slave-like. Every girl at some time, whoever she may be, has a prince charming to dream of. Arthur's dark good looks, smooth dark hair and trimmed moustache, added to a straight athletic build, could easily fit him out for the role of a Rajput warrior in times of chivalry.

Shanti, after a while, became less shy, or perhaps apprehensive, of Arthur. She had a sitar, and Arthur thought he heard her singing once or twice.

In fact, she saw more of Arthur than he knew, for Shanti, on silent feet, was good at looking round corners.

After about three weeks of the new regime, it was evident that the lighter showers of rain were becoming the monsoon proper and Arthur took what looked like being his last morning range round on Kumar.

Watching the clouds, he thought to himself that he had gone far enough and started back faster than usual to avoid a likely downpour. He hung his topee by its strap on the saddle the better to see where he was going and took a short cut between two paths. Then, for a moment, he looked the wrong way.

A protruding dead branch cracked him painfully hard on the side of his head above the eye. Half-stunned, he reined Kumar in, and then he felt the warm blood running down his cheek. He dared not dismount, but, recovering his senses, he managed to tie a handkerchief round his head and wove his way back on to the path he knew.

Half a mile from the bungalow the heavens opened, and with steam rising from Kumar's sides he made a bedraggled return and, thankfully handing Kumar over to the waiting, and shocked, syce, he left for the washroom and surveyed his face in the mirror.

A bad gash, beginning to clot, but re-opened by the rain, confronted him. He pressed a handful of cotton wool to it. Not a chance to get stitches, he thought; four or five would do it. After another pad of cotton wool the bleeding stopped.

Motiram, lingering in the doorway, came forward.

"Sahib, you need doctor?" he queried.

"No, Motiram, it is not very bad, but I must lie down," Lane replied. "Don't make 'nasta', my breakfast, but go and tell Robert's sahib I cannot come down to-day, but tomorrow all right."

"Ha-ji, Sahib."

Arthur's head was beginning to swell a bit, and ached. He lay down on his bed.

This time Shanti did not hesitate. She came right in.

Arthur waved away the bowl she carried.

"No, Shanti, no water," he said, and shut his eyes.

Shanti came and sat on the bed and put her soft hand above Arthur's forehead.

He kept his eyes shut, not trusting himself to open them. Shanti was making soothing noises, musical and quiet. He felt her arm slip behind him to rearrange his pillow.

Arthur might not have chosen it this way; he had racked his brains as to how to bring it about, but now the opening had been made. He took Shanti's other hand in his.

She hurried to the kitchen before Motiram should get back and made coffee and toast which Arthur had, and felt better for it. He decided to make the most of his situation.

Motiram returned and said that Percy Roberts would look in later, but Shanti had no intention of leaving Arthur then.

She was there when Percy and Edna Roberts arrived, but moved away quickly on hearing the car. Edna's presence deterred Percy from making any ribald remark.

"Now I told you to look out for branches, didn't I?" he said, "thank God you didn't fall off."

"Not Kumar's fault either," Arthur managed to say, wincing. "I'll be all right tomorrow, it's too high for a black eye."

"I'll send you up something soft like a stew, in a tiffin carrier this evening," Edna offered, sympathetically.

"I guess he is in good hands now," Percy had to say.

"I would like that, Edna, sorry to be a nuisance," Arthur said.

After Shanti came back and sat down again on his bed,

Arthur held her however and whenever he could, and everywhere he touched he felt her warm, firm softness. She did not leave him, helping him to have Edna's meal, until dark and by then, for both of them, it could only be a prelude.

Arthur taught Shanti some English as the days moved on. He told her about 'Darling' and what it meant, and loved to hear her say it. The split above his eye took about a week to close up properly and, without any stitches, mended nicely. It had served its purpose well.

About that time Shanti came to him one night and slipped under his mosquito net. Arthur was not sure about Indian night garb, but Shanti's was uncomplicated, a voluminous nightie in effect, with short baggy bloomers under it. She took the first off herself and snuggled beside Arthur soon making him almost mad with desire.

The wonder of her silky body and firm young breasts with sepia tips seemed to envelop him as in a sanctuary tinged with the faint perfume of jasmine.

Shanti was breathing into his ear and nibbled the lobe, her fingers digging into the muscles of his arms as he held her.

Arthur tried to think how Shanti, in her virginity, might prepare herself for the act of sexual love with him. He could not, not him, throw her on her back, tear at her undergarment. He buried his head between her breasts and slid one hand down to caress a velvet buttock. With the other, at the end of his tether, he guided one of hers between his legs.

Almost crying in blessed relief and for joy, Arthur slept. Once when he awoke, Shanti was there, tucked at the edge of the bed. She seemed awake and drew closer when he touched her, but the next time, nearer daybreak, she was gone.

Arthur marvelled at a woman like Shanti, unversed up to then in love, yet sweet, natural and quite uninhibited. He realised that this was far from mere concubinage and that he was deeply in love.

In her way too, Shanti could not be more obsessed with Arthur. Now acquiescent in all that he had taught her of the acts of love, when they were alone she had dropped the 'sahib' and called him by his name.

Work had now taken the railway line out of sight from Percy Roberts' home and headquarters, but there was still no point in moving on. Some of Roberts' men were bivouacking further along now that the monsoon had rained itself out.

Arthur would never forget that monsoon. Nights when, during a break in the showers, Shanti would come out of the darkness to him, and hardly had he put his book down before, nakedly, she pulled at his sarong and enfolded him with her satin arms and legs as if not to let any part of him escape.

Later, as they would lie in a half-embrace listening to the rain torrenting down, she would say again: "Atur, 'dalling,' I love you."

The sensuous warmth of closeness heightened by being secure from the storm while yet its witness, seemed to Arthur the nearest he could be to heaven on earth.

"Oh Shanti, so do I love you," was the only spoken thought of his reply.

Each night such as that could only be cured in sleep, and sometimes, alone when he awoke, Arthur, for a moment, seemed to come out of a dream; except that he never remembered his actual dreams.

It is strange, he thought, that like a drug, the ecstasy of lovers together so soon passes away, and when eagerly renewed that, too soon, seemed brief. Unlike pain which lasts until its cause is healed. Unlike an addiction too, as each partner is a separate being and when one is gone only a longing that has no palliative lingers for a while.

As he carried on with his diminishing task, Arthur comforted himself by thinking that Ajmer was not so far away and naturally, he could be expected to come over to Udaipur occasionally to check how things were going.

Percy Roberts had, perhaps surprisingly, been restrained in his comments about Shanti. Arthur Lane's contented demeanour since about the time of his riding accident had been there for all to see, and coincidentally his evening meals with the Roberts' had fallen off.

Having taken credit for Shanti's arrival via her mother, Nanabhai, who visited the Inspection bungalow about once a week to see how her daughter was coping, Percy was surprised himself at the favour he had done Arthur.

The monsoon, Arthur found, was not so intensive as down in Bombay on the coast. Work on the railway line was little affected.

By the beginning of October Percy estimated that Arthur was safe in suggesting to Ainsley that he could wind up his assignment in two or three weeks.

"What will you do then, Percy?" Arthur asked.'

"Oh, I can start laying off some of the men, starting with the coolies from Udaipur," Percy replied, "but I have to stick around for some time yet until rolling stock comes through and the line is tested."

"Don't you feel jealous?" he added.

Arthur knew he meant Shanti, but he ignored the

innuendo. "No, I am ready to get back and work on the merchandise and passenger factors," he said.

Roberts had the sense to see that, with Arthur, the subject of Shanti was definitely not one for chattiness.

A formal parting from Shanti was impossible.

"I must soon stop living here, my Shanti." Arthur told her, "but I will come back many times and see you."

Shanti clung to him and he felt her tears.

"Really, do not cry, Shanti," he implored her. Yet in his heart Arthur knew that India was not like South East Asia or the Pacific Islands where a dusky maiden might wait for a roving white lover, and eventually, maybe marry him.

Shanti accepted that when Arthur left the bungalow she would return to her people and soon, as Nanabhai was planning, make that good marriage for which she was now so much better equipped.

Arthur might try, of this she was sure, but he would not find her ever again alone, and if she too tried, Motiram, in Nanabhai's confidence, would certainly defame her.

Arthur did try. How could he leave this most wonderful love without having any hope or expectation that it could be renewed?

His first visit was for the official opening of the line with dignitaries from Bombay, Delhi and Udaipur, though not the Maharana himself. From his stand he could not deviate. Arthur was complimented, and Percy Roberts too, whom he managed to take aside.

"Percy, this is all the spit and polish as we know, and I have got to spend a week here after all these people have dispersed, to report on the ways and means. Do fix me up in the Inspection bungalow. My bearer, Lalji, got back all right to Ajmer, but I have left him behind."

"Surely I will, there is still no Forest officer coming to these parts," said Percy. "No problem."

When he returned to the bungalow Arthur Lane had been away from the Udaipur line two months and he hardly knew how he had weathered them.

Motiram was there, smiling broadly. "Salaam, Lane sahib," he said, and looking very pleased with himself, he indicated the surrounds of the bungalow which were alive with flowers, fostered by the rains, and the fact that Motiram had had no visitors to look after other than friends who called, including, it seemed, Nanabhai.

"Bahut achha, Motiram, bahut achha kam." Lane did agree that he had worked well.

Motiram was going to make the best of the week with the money from Roberts sahib to stock up the food, but Lane was gloomy, remembering all too vividly his last night there with Shanti. Did she know of his arrival; would she come? These were the only thoughts that meant anything to him.

Of course he had to ask Motiram about her, trying all he could to sound offhand.

"Ha-ji, sahib," Motiram assured him. "Nanabhai will come tomorrow to see you and tell you the news that her daughter, Shanti, is betrothed to the eldest son of a rich grain merchant in the bazaar."

Arthur felt as if he had been clubbed. So what Shanti had said in her tears was true.

Sure enough, Nanabhai, bursting with pride, and in her best sari, was there when Arthur returned up the hill. She confirmed what Motiram had revealed already.

From the folds of her garments Nanabhai drew out what she said was a greeting from Shanti to Arthur. It did not, could not, really speak, but it was a talisman of hers that he recognised, painted round with intertwined flowers, vine-like, bamboo trunks and leaves, but within it all he could make out a word. The word was 'Atur.'

Shanti's wedding, a grand affair, the dowry for which would leave Nanabhai's family almost penniless for many a day, she said, would be within a month, on the correct propitious day.

Men are naturally inclined to put a time limit on their love affairs, but suddenly to know that at the height of its joy an idyllic period of one's life has ended is liable to cause a wound that is permanent.

Arthur did not know how he managed to stay in the bungalow for six days. He thought of Kumar and went to see him in Percy Roberts' stable. He ate on several nights with the Roberts, besides a couple of lunches.

Percy said little, apart from matters only to do with the job in hand, but Arthur was aware of him studying his face as well as wearing an air of sympathy.

"I hear you could be going back to Bombay before long," Percy ventured. "You will be glad now, eh?"

Arthur looked at him directly. "Of course I knew it had to come, Percy. Not the transfer back exactly, but what it would mean leaving even Ajmer. But now, I can't be glad. I've got to have time to get over how I feel inside, I suppose."

Percy could only change the subject. How could I know, he thought, that Nanabhai's daughter could be that beautiful and tie Arthur Lane up into such a knot. Any sort of banter was out of the question now.

"You'll put in a good word for me, and give a thought to Edna and me when you are in Bombay again?" he asked.

"Yes, Percy, of course I will, and I shall mean it." Arthur said.

Back in Ajmer throughout the Cold Weather, Arthur was restless and haunted by the comparative nearness of Udaipur, knowing that Shanti was unattainable. There were no seasonable diversions that he could plunge into as in Bombay.

He bought a horse, a remount that could be spared by the 6th D.C.O. Lancers at Kotah who were moving up to Mooltan. A four-year-old Australian waler mare who he called 'Kumari,' and spent every morning training her before breakfast, first lunging, then long reining with the saddle on.

Kumari soon took to having a rider, and half-way through the Cold Weather Arthur was able to guide her on to forest trails and recapture some of the peace that he knew roving the jungle slopes above the Inspection bungalow by Udaipur.

It was not much longer until he had been four years with the Company and he set off on his first home leave.

On his return in October, he was met by the Assistant General Manager of the B.B. & C.I., one Simon Owen, whom he knew slightly.

Escorting Lane to the office Owen told him: "Lane, we are keeping you in Bombay, you may have guessed this."

"Well, I knew it was coming before I went on leave," Arthur replied, "but I didn't know when. I did not pack up all my things in Ajmer."

"Don't worry, Ainsley had them all packed up and sent down to us. I don't think you'll find anything missing, but let me know in due course."

"You did a nice job in Udaipur," Owen continued, causing Arthur to catch his breath, but Owen went on blandly. "We have also, you will be pleased to hear, acted on your recommendation not to ease off on Surat and are glad to have your engineering designs and work programmes from Ajmer. Your job here is deputy to the Chief Engineer, Jackson."

Arthur had allowed Udaipur to fade in the utterly contrasting atmosphere of 1920s Britain, but on the ship he had hoped fervently to be able to stay in Bombay.

He settled down to an absorbing task and also to the full and varied life of the 'First City in India,' interspersed with inspection trips to all the area covered directly by the B.B. & C.I.'s Head Office.

Finally, Arthur Lane climbed right up the ladder.

Denis Fairbairn, after he had come on the scene, was grateful for Arthur Lane's friendship and confidences, though the most important one was never known to have been divulged to anyone.

To some chokrahs, old koi hais were, if not a bore, something of a sad joke until they themselves had savoured or endured the many unanticipated things that life in India bestowed, or foisted, upon them.

On his second home leave, Denis Fairbairn determined to try and look up Arthur Lane, now retired, but somehow what with family ties and a girl he met on the boat home, he did not make it. He heard that Lane had married an amiable and competent childless widow of about his own age. So Lane evidently never got involved with any children.

They lived somewhere in Surrey or Sussex, or was it Hampshire?

# GLOSSARY OF INDIAN NAMES

| | |
|---|---|
| Achha Lai | That's fine |
| Bandobast | Arrangement or programme. (eg) for an outing, travel, or a party. |
| Bearer | Personal servant and butler. |
| Bhat | Speech or language. |
| Boxwallah | One whose job involves working in an office. |
| Burra sahib | The Boss. |
| Chitti | A note or short letter. |
| Chowkidar | Watchman. |
| Chokrah | Literally a young boy. A junior employee. |
| Chota hazri | Early morning tea. |
| Chota peg | A small drink. Usually whiskey. |
| Chummery | A shared bachelor residence. |
| Dak Bungalow | Remote rest house notably for postal (dak) runners. |

| | |
|---|---|
| Dharzi | Tailor. |
| Dhobi | Washerman. |
| Dusra | Another. |
| Fishing fleet | Eligible ladies out for the social season. |
| Jheel | Large pond or small lake in countryside |
| Khansama | Housekeeper/cook. |
| Kutcha | Poor quality. |
| Maidan | Public open space in or near town. |
| Mullokh | Home village |
| Munshi | Teacher. |
| Nimbu pani | Fresh lime and water with ice. |
| Nullah | Stream bed; very often dry. |
| Numdah | Soft woollen cloth used under saddles. |
| Pucca | Good quality. |

| | |
|---|---|
| Puggree | Turban or headcloth. |
| Puja | A prayer or religious offering. |
| Rishi | A learned holy man. |
| Saddhu | A religious ascetic, often ash-covered. |
| Shikar | Wild game hunting. |
| Syce | Native Groom for horses. |

\* \* \*